Newton Crosland

Stories of the City of London

Retold for Youthful Readers

Newton Crosland

Stories of the City of London
Retold for Youthful Readers

ISBN/EAN: 9783744750516

Printed in Europe, USA, Canada, Australia, Japan

Cover: Foto ©Andreas Hilbeck / pixelio.de

More available books at **www.hansebooks.com**

STORIES

OF

THE CITY OF LONDON

Retold for Youthful Readers.

BY

MRS. NEWTON CROSLAND.

AUTHOR OF "HUBERT FREETH'S PROSPERITY," "MEMORABLE WOMEN," ETC.

ILLUSTRATED BY

ALFRED T. ELWES AND JOHN JELLICERE.

> " Our crowded town,
> Whose age is poetry. . . . .
> Present and Past
> Alike impregnate London's ' cloud-capp'd towers '
> With Poesy's own soul. . . . .
> Oh ! not blind
> To Nature's loveliness are they who still
> May love the Regal City. . . . ."

LONDON:

W.. H. ALLEN & CO., 13, WATERLOO PLACE, S.W.

PUBLISHERS TO THE INDIA OFFICE.

1880.

LONDON:
PRINTED BY WOODFALL AND KINDER,
MILFORD LANE, STRAND, W.C.

PREFACE.

I AM well aware that each of the following Stories either has been or might be made the subject of a separate instructive volume; but elaborations of History, with all their wide-spread ramifications, are only really acceptable to the mature and already well-informed reader. To the young there must ever be a gradual acquirement of all sorts of knowledge, and those histories which are most diffuse, and those biographies which are most ample, do not always make the deepest impression on youthful minds. Remembering this, my aim has been to retell these true stories graphically, yet succinctly; believing that interest may be maintained through forty pages when it would flag under a more prolonged effort, and knowing that it is that in which we are really interested which the memory retains most faithfully.

C. C.

BLACKHEATH, *December*, 1880.

CONTENTS.

ILLUSTRATIONS.

STORIES

OF

THE CITY OF LONDON.

LONDON BRIDGE.

SUPPOSE there are very few English people who do not know London Bridge, either by actual observation or by means of pictorial representation. But often things that are very familiar to us awaken little thought in our minds, and among the multitude of passengers who cross the Thames every day by means of London Bridge, perhaps only a few reflect on the re-

markable events with which the spot is associated. Everybody, no doubt, observes the
ceaseless traffic which is going on, and finds
time to notice the shipping which crowds the
river below bridge, and the wharves which
are the scene of so much bustling business;
while on both sides of the bridge there may
be seen steamboats darting along or bend-
ing their funnels to pass through the arches.
Weather even makes but little difference, for
the people who congregate near London Bridge
are for the most part intent on pursuits which
must not be hindered by heat or cold, or rain or
drought. Perhaps they are too busy to pause
and think of times so different from the present
that it requires a strong effort of the imagination
to picture them.

Think of a London not a twentieth part
the size it is at present. Think of a London
without carriages or cabs or omnibuses, and
with only a few wheeled vehicles of a rude
description: of a London not lighted at night,
and with streets of houses built chiefly of wood,
the upper floors of which projected far over the

pathway. No doubt you have seen pictures of such houses, if not the houses themselves, for in many old cities a few of them still remain. They must have been rather convenient to protect passengers in wet weather, for in those olden days nobody dreamed of such a thing as an umbrella; but the overhanging stories must have made the shops beneath them very dark, especially as the streets were usually narrow.

In the old time every shop had a sign, generally descriptive of its character, and for the good reason that very few people could read. Thus, when a serving-man was sent on an errand by his master, he was very glad to know that the sign of a lamb suspended by its body, just as you may see it in the order of the Golden Fleece, meant that the shopkeeper was a hosier and dealer in many woollen articles; that a pestle and mortar indicated an apothecary; a striped pole a barber-surgeon—so called because the barber drew teeth and bled people; or a bunch of grapes a vintner; and so on with many trades. Other houses were designated by what may be called fancy signs, such as a blue boar, a red lion, a black bull, a spread eagle, or a swan.

But even in the days long preceding these mediæval, or middle ages, people dwelt on the banks of the Thames, and must have needed to pass often from one shore to the other; and though nothing is known quite positively on the subject, there is reason to believe that the first bridge across the river was built either by the Romans, or by the natives shortly after the Romans left England. There are still to be traced the remains of the great Roman Road which ran across the whole country from the south-east to the north-west coast, and its name is still perpetuated where it passed through London as Watling Street.

Now, originally this road appears to have reached the Thames at Westminster, where the water was shallow; for in those old days that neighbourhood was very much of a swamp, and what is now St. James's Park was a tidal lagoon; that is to say, at high tide a great pond formed there. It was where the channel of the stream grew narrower that the water naturally became deeper. If, as it seems, the Roman Road was in the first instance brought to Westminster, we may imagine that travellers on it had some means of crossing the river at that point; perhaps they used a ferry-boat, though some antiquaries have believed that the stream just there was often, if not always, shallow enough to be fordable. A street in the district still bears the name of Horseferry Road.

But an uncertain, tedious, and inconvenient mode of travelling was not a thing that either the Romans or the British were inclined to endure longer than they could help; and it seems tolerably clear that one or the other looked about for the most convenient place at which either to build a bridge or establish a ferry, and that finally they selected pretty nearly the spot on which London Bridge now rests. One thing we know, and that is, that they diverted the Roman Road from Westminster, making a sharp turn at Tyburn—near where is now the Marble Arch—and carrying it straight to what is at present called Newgate. From this spot it ran across the city diagonally nearly through the modern Watling Street before it reached the river.

Now it is not at all likely that the Romans would have taken this trouble if they had not wanted to cross the Thames in some way more pleasant than by a ford; for at the spot the road now reached the stream was much deeper than at Westminster, though on the other hand narrower, and every way more suitable for building a bridge. It is highly probable, however, that they first established a Ferry.

There still remains a church called St. Mary's Overy near the foot of the present London Bridge, and there is little doubt that Overy is but a corruption of "over the Ferry." It stands on the site of what was at first a Nunnery, and afterwards a college for Priests. The story goes that the Ferry brought considerable profit to the Ferryman and his wife, who left all they had, and the right they must have obtained over the Ferry, to their only daughter, who was the original builder of the religious house. When it came into the hands of the priests they seem to have been rich enough to build a wooden bridge, and afterwards keep it for a length of time in repair.

Probably, however, it was not a very substantial one that was erected, for we find that in A.D. 993, a Norwegian fleet sailed up the river as far as Staines, which could not have been the case had there been a bridge to impede its course. However, soon after this time some sort of bridge was erected, though like its predecessor not destined to last; for we learn that in A.D. 1008 there was a battle of London Bridge, in which Olave, the Norwegian king—who was helping Ethelred the Unready to fight against the Danes—with his ships and Norsemen entirely destroyed it. No doubt the fabric was of wood or it could not have given way, though the plan for its destruction was ingenious. The Norwegians chose the time of the ebbing tide to help them, lashed their own vessels with strong cables to the piers, and then plied their oars with their utmost strength, though the Danes, who had possession of the bridge, hurled stones and other missiles on them from above. But at last it fell with a great crash, plunging its defenders in the water, and a great number of them were drowned.

Yet another and another slight bridge seem to have been erected; for one certainly existed when Canute invaded England in A.D. 1016, as he had to cut a channel for his ships in the low marshy land by the river's side, taking them round by its means from Rotherhithe to Chelsea; and also we find that in November, 1091, in the reign of William Rufus, a tremendous storm, which was accompanied by a high tide of immense force, swept the bridge entirely away. Another bridge, likewise of wood, was burnt down in 1136, when a destructive fire raged in London.

The London Bridge, however, with which we have chiefly to do, and which was most rich in historical associations, was far more durable than its predecessors. It was the first one built of stone, and was begun in the reign of Henry the Second and finished in that of King John. The architect was Peter, surnamed Colechurch— it is to be presumed because he was curate of St. Mary's Colechurch. In those times learning and skill in the arts and sciences were almost wholly confined to the monks, and therefore there was nothing unusual in one of them being an architect. The cost of this new erection was so great, that a tax laid upon wool was the chief means to defray it; hence arose the joke that London Bridge was built upon woolpacks. Of course the people who lived at the time, and perhaps their children and grand-children, understood the saying; but after a while its peculiar meaning was forgotten, and the words were taken in a literal sense. We can easily understand, if we really think about it, how facts must have been forgotten or misstated when there were no printed books to read, and when only a very few people could read and write at all; after old persons who knew the truth of things were dead, all about them was merely hearsay, except indeed the written records kept by learned people, and to which historians are so largely indebted.

Peter Colechurch did not live to see his fine stone bridge quite finished, though he super-intended the work for nearly thirty years, and no doubt it was completed exactly in the manner he had planned. It consisted of 20 arches, was raised 60 feet from the river, was 40 feet wide from parapet to parapet, and was 926 feet in length.

As for hundreds of years to come, that is to say until the middle of the eighteenth century, there was only this one bridge over the Thames, we can fancy how constantly it was thronged by passengers; and no doubt it was for this reason that it was considered a capital place for business, as all great thoroughfares to this day are. Probably it was for the good opportunity of displaying wares and tempting purchasers that the custom arose of building houses on bridges that spanned the rivers near which great cities were founded, and the London Bridge of the middle ages formed no exception to the rule. Tall houses of many stories were speedily built upon it; and though overhanging floors, such as I have already described, projected far beyond the shop fronts below, the roadway of forty feet must still have been considerably narrowed.

In the centre of the bridge, over the tenth pier, was erected a chapel, dedicated to St. Thomas à Becket, and here Peter Colechurch, the priest and architect, was buried. This chapel was on the east side of the bridge, and to support it the central pier on which it stood was carried farther out to the east than the others. It must have been a beautiful building, with a frontage of thirty feet. The interior consisted of a chapel proper, and a crypt beneath it, the latter having a flight of stairs to the river, as well as easy means of communication with the chapel and the street. The crypt was about twenty feet in height, supported by clustered columns of great beauty; and both chapel and crypt were lighted by arched windows looking out on the river.

In the street of houses which the bridge speedily became there were three breaks—openings to the water—and between the chapel and the Southwark end of the bridge, one of the arches was formed by a drawbridge. Evidently the citizens had it in their minds to defend London Bridge if necessary, and prevent the advance of foes.   At the north end of the draw-bridge was a tower, on which the heads of persons executed for high treason were exposed—a ghastly and barbarous practice, all the more shocking to contemplate because in those times of frequent civil discord, when might often prevailed over right, many great and good men were called traitors and suffered accordingly.

Towards the close of the sixteenth century, this tower was replaced by so singular an edifice, that it was called Nonsuch House.   It was entirely of wood, and was said to have been constructed in Holland, sent over to England in pieces, and put up here with only wooden pegs to hold it together.   It extended right across the bridge by means of an archway, and its east and west gables protruded far beyond the line of the bridge.   At each of the four corners was a short dome with a spire and gilded vane, so that something of this fantastic building could be seen from any quarter.

When Nonsuch House was erected the traitors' heads withering on pikes were removed to the gateway at the Southwark end of the bridge,

which for this reason acquired the name of
"Traitors' Gate."

To have a true notion of old London Bridge
we need to remember a great many things. We
must think of it as the only bridge across the
Thames, and consequently as always thronged;
we must think of the tall houses with their
swinging signs, rattling in the wind; of the
overhanging stories, approaching the opposite
ones so nearly that neighbours must often have
chatted with each other from their lattices. We
must think of the droves of oxen and flocks of
sheep coming from the country to feed the town;
of the waggons and pack horses constantly going
to and fro; and later on, when coaches were introduced, of the very fine but cumbrous carriages
of the nobility and rich people who had to cross
the bridge in many of their journeys, and who
also were fond of coming to London Bridge to do
their shopping. Often their great coaches were
drawn by four horses, partly on account of the
great weight the animals had to draw, and partly
on account of the general badness of country
roads.

As for pedestrians, they must have come badly off; for there was no footpath, and the safest place was to walk behind some heavy vehicle. I do not fancy there was much need to run to keep up with anything—especially the laden waggons—for the bridge was usually so crowded that no one passed along very fast. I suppose brisk horsemen who could thread their way in and out had the best of it. In picturing this daily life of the bridge we must not forget the ghastly heads set upon the Bridge Tower and afterwards on Traitors' Gate, and left to rot in the rain and wind and sunshine. The head of the Scottish hero William Wallace, and that of the grey-haired Earl of Northumberland, the father of Hotspur, were here exposed; and later on, in the reign of Henry the Eighth, the remains of Fisher, Bishop of Rochester, and Sir Thomas More—both executed for refusing to acknowledge the king's spiritual supremacy— were subjected to the same revolting indignity.

Months after the exposure of Sir Thomas More's head, and when it was about to be thrown into the Thames to make way for the

head of some other unfortunate, that of Sir
Thomas was purchased by his daughter Margaret, whose pious devotion to her father is well
known to students of history and biography.
The story goes that it was found hardly changed
at all, except, indeed, that "the hairs of his head
being almost grey before his martyrdom, they
seemed now as it were reddish or yellow." For
hundreds of years the custom of exposing human heads in this manner prevailed, and there
are old prints remaining which show them,
sometimes as many as thirty at a time, we are
told, having been seen. Even as late as after
the Restoration the heads of some of the Regi-
cides were set up on London Bridge.

The citizens of London no doubt from the
first determined to make all possible use of their
bridge; and often enough they took the law
into their own hands. An account is given of
the manner in which they prevented Queen
Eleanor of Provence, the wife of Henry the
Third, from passing along the river to Windsor,
where she wished to take shelter. She was hated
by the English for her many selfish and unprin-

cipled acts, though she was called La Belle for her beauty, and was accomplished in the graceful arts. She had been living for some time in the Tower with her husband, they having taken refuge there from the fury of the Barons ; but, tired of the seclusion, she determined to chance what might happen, and reside at Windsor. The royal barge was sumptuously prepared, and she had a fit retinue in attendance, and as she took the seat of state, trumpets signalled her departure. But at the bridge her passage was stopped. A crowd of Londoners had assembled on it, and they so assaulted her with stones and dirt—and we must add foul language—that she had to turn back.

A century later there was another memorable scene on London Bridge when Wat Tyler and his Kentish men forced their way into the city, notwithstanding the vigorous efforts of the Lord Mayor, Sir William Walworth, to resist them. The drawbridge was raised up and fastened by a great chain of iron, but the commons of Surrey prevailed with the wardens to let it down, under threat of destroying them

altogether if they refused. It would indeed be
a long history to tell of the stirring events and
processions of which London Bridge was for
centuries the scene.

Being the direct entrance to the metropolis
from the southern or south-eastern coast, foreign
princesses who came to be English Queens, notable visitors from distant lands, and sometimes
famous captives, all traversed the bridge in more
or less state. On London Bridge Henry the
Fifth was received in triumph after his victory
at Agincourt—that " Harry the King " of whom
Shakespeare writes so finely—and whose dead
body, seven years later, was borne along this
same highway with funereal splendour.

When travelling was so much more difficult
than it is at present, people made home the scene
of their chief pleasures. Merchants and traders
for the most part lived at their places of business, and must have been rich indeed before they
thought of country houses; nor did they want
them for health's sake as much as they do now.
There was not any part of London in those old
times that was far from green fields and rural

c

scenery, and the dwellers on London Bridge often resorted to Finsbury Fields for exercise and pastimes. Finsbury now is in the very heart of the east part of London, but three hundred years ago what we now call athletic sports were carried on there—men leaping and wrestling, casting the stone, and shooting with the long bow. Also the Londoners had much amusement on the Thames, which was then a clear silvery stream, rich in fish and gay with boats and barges, people using it as a highway from one end of London to the other.

No doubt the pleasantest rooms in the London Bridge houses were those which faced the river. In bright weather there was always sunshine on them some part of the day, and there was always some moving river scene to look out upon. And for profit as well as amusement a fish-pond was constructed in connection with the bridge, by which the fish caught in it at high tide were prevented by an iron railing from returning to the river.

The apprentice boys of the reign of Henry

the Eighth were for the most part a rough and unruly set, but there is a pretty story told of one of them that had important consequences. His name was Edward Osborne, and he was apprenticed to William Hewet, a thriving clothworker living on London Bridge. Hewet had a little daughter—an only child—who when about the age of four years fell from her nurse's arms out of a window into the river. Edward Osborne, then a mere lad of twelve or fourteen, happening to be on the spot, without a moment's hesitation jumped into the water, and succeeded, though not without difficulty, in saving the child. In consequence of the numerous arches the water was always rough at London Bridge, with waves more or less like those of the ocean, and with dangerous eddies caused by the obstructions the rushing river found. So much was this the case that at certain stages of the tide it was thought positively dangerous to attempt the passage of a wherry beneath the bridge. Thus you see it was a particularly ugly place at which to be immersed. The fall, too, must have been from a considerable height, and the leap of the brave boy probably not less so, and we may be sure he deserved all the praise that was showered upon him for the rescue.

When we read stories of this kind it is a good plan to try and picture the scene, and imagine much that must have happened. We can fancy the father's joy that his darling Anne—that was her name—was saved, and his grateful acknowledgments to the 'prentice lad who had risked his own life to preserve that of the little girl; and I do not think we should be far wrong in picturing the careless servant with a white face of terror, and apron to her eyes, shedding floods of tears and being soundly scolded.

As for Edward Osborne—himself half drowned—no doubt he was sent to bed and cosited just the same as the little girl was, and made much of as he had never been before; and when he quite recovered from the shock he had received he must have found himself the hero of the bridge, all the apprentices thronging about him and seeming proud to be considered his friends. When we remember his after

career there is good reason to suppose that
Osborne was a very superior lad, and probably
his master had already discovered his good
qualities ; but however this may have been it
is certain that as he grew up he was treated
like a son by the worthy cloth-worker in whose
house he lived continually.

William Hewet prospered in his business so
much that in a few years he became a very
wealthy man, and lived to receive the honour of
knighthood and be Lord Mayor of London.
Meanwhile, his daughter, Mistress Anne, as she
was called, grew to be a very charming girl, and
as she was looked upon as a rich heiress was
sought in marriage by people of consequence a
great many times. But her father had no doubt
studied the character of Edward Osborne, and
observed the attachment which had sprung up
between him and the child he had rescued.
Certain it is that Hewet gave his daughter in
marriage to the young apprentice with hearty
good will, saying he " had saved her, and he
should have her."

In due time Edward Osborne became quite as

wealthy and distinguished a man as his father-in-law had been, and was himself knighted, and chosen Lord Mayor of London in the reign of Queen Elizabeth.   No doubt his children were worthy of their parentage, and indeed his family and their descendants so prospered in life and advanced in social position that the great-grand-son of Sir Edward and Anne Osborne was the first Duke of Leeds, from whom all the succeeding Dukes have descended.

It was in the reign of Queen Elizabeth that some very famous and ingenious waterworks were erected at the Middlesex side of London Bridge.   They were invented by a Dutchman—a "free denizen" he was called—for the purpose of supplying the City with water, and were in the first instance moved only by the tide passing through the first arch, but subsequently the watercourses of some other arches were diverted and turned into rapids to keep the wheels in motion.   We can imagine how great a boon these works must have been to Londoners, who, hitherto, when a little distant from the banks of the Thames, had been mainly dependent on wells or ditches like rivulets for their supply of water. These works—though often repaired and improved—continued in operation till 1822, when an act of Parliament was passed for their removal. By this time London had a purer supply of water than could be obtained by these means, and besides, preparations were being made for pulling down the old bridge.

Durable as London Bridge was, it could not last for ever, and it had had many trials to go through, besides suffering from the slow work of time. Four times a portion of it was destroyed by fire, namely—in 1212, when historians say not less than three thousand persons perished in consequence of being caught between the masses of flame. They had assembled on the bridge to see the fire which, having spread from the Church of St. Mary over to the Southwark gate of the bridge, was suddenly carried by the wind to the London end. No doubt many of these unfortunates dropped into the river and were drowned, and the scene must have been nearly as terrible as that of a burning ship on the ocean. In February 1663 a fire broke out

from the carelessness of a servant placing some
hot coals under a flight of stairs, a fire which
raged many hours, destroying all the houses on
the bridge from the north end to the first opening—one of the breaks already described by
which passengers could see the river. These
houses were not all rebuilt when the great fire of
1666 devastated London, and though it did not
make its way quite across the bridge, it again
reduced to ashes all the houses on both sides as
far as the first opening. Again, as late as 1725,
the bridge was the scene of a dreadful fire, which
consumed nearly sixty houses, and so injured
the old Traitors' Gate, that what remained of it
had to be pulled down, and the gate entirely
rebuilt. No doubt, on all these occasions the
free current of air afforded by the river fanned
the flames and greatly added to their force.

The bridge also had many trials from storm
and frost, one of the most notable having been
in January 1281, when five of the arches were
carried away, either by the action of the ice, or
the swell of the river which happened in consequence of severe frost. No wonder that in its

long existence of more than six hundred years
London Bridge was subjected to so many repairs
and modifications that, could Peter Colechurch
have looked at it, he would hardly have recognized his own work—yet still we are justified in calling it his as long as the structure
lasted.

Early, however, in the eighteenth century, the
narrowness of the thoroughfare became a great
inconvenience. Population, and consequently
traffic, were increasing, and in 1757 the work of
pulling down the houses was begun. It was
carried on slowly, probably out of consideration
for the rights of householders, and the Southwark gate remained standing till 1766.

An old writer describes from his own recollec-
tion the street on London Bridge—" narrow,
darksome and dangerous," with "frequent arches
of timber crossing from the tops of the houses
to keep them together, and from falling into the
river." In one of Hogarth's pictures which is
to be seen in the National Gallery, there is a
view of Old London Bridge with houses upon it
that look ready to topple over. Though it was

high time that the houses should be taken down, we can fancy the bridge was a picturesque object to artists. Indeed, it is believed that more than one painter of note fitted up a studio on the bridge, the most famous of them having been Hans Holbein. The houses looking east and west, sunrise or sunset upon the river must often have been a lovely sight from them; while running water, with all the variation of the tides—and made a highway with boats and barges, and frequent State processions—must have presented endless scenes of interest to a painter's eye.

Venerable as Old London Bridge was, and endeared to the citizens from its many stirring associations, its days, however, were numbered. Early in the present century it was found to be incapable of satisfactory repair, and in 1822 an Act of Parliament was passed for the erection of a new bridge, which is the present one. Strange to say, the Corporation of the City of London were violently opposed to the measure, wishing still only to repair the old structure. Happily wiser counsels prevailed, the design chosen for a new bridge being that of the engineer John

Rennie. He, however, died before the work was begun, though it was superintended by his son. The first pile of the first coffer-dam was driven on the 15th of March, 1824; the foundation stone was laid on the 15th of June, 1825, and the bridge was opened by King William the Fourth and Queen Adelaide, August 1, 1831. The occasion was made a great holiday and gala day in London, as many elderly people can still well remember.

The 1st of August was the anniversary of the accession of the house of Hanover, and very probably for that reason it was selected for the ceremony. It was a lovely summer day, still and warm. The King and Queen went, with their retinue, in State barges from Somerset House. The King, though an old man, ascended the long flight of steps from the river without apparent fatigue, and amid loud cheers from the crowd. The customary formality of presenting the keys of the city by the Lord Mayor was gone through—they being, of course, graciously returned by the King—and the royal party proceeded to a splendid pavilion which had been erected on the new bridge. After inspecting the bridge, and having had its structure explained, they returned to the pavilion, where a sumptuous banquet was prepared for them.

The Lord Mayor proposed the health of the King, and the King drank out of a gold cup to the prosperity and commerce of the City of London. Many other "toasts" were given, according to the custom at public banquets, and "drinking healths" prevailed in those days to a great extent.

After the banquet the royal party returned to Somerset House by water, and the Lord Mayor and the City Companies followed in their State barges gaily decorated. It was a great show, that reminded spectators of much older times.

The present bridge stands about 180 feet higher up the river than its predecessor, and consequently more westward; and, of course, the old bridge was left standing until the new one was brought into use. But the ancient structure had long been considered positively insecure, and timid people in heavy vehicles

passed over it in fear and trembling. The new
bridge already seems old to the generation
which has arisen since its erection, and it has
been the high road by which many famous
people have entered London—as it is the daily
scene of enormous traffic. But perhaps no day
in its history is more memorable than the 7th
of March, 1863, when it was decorated with
the insignia of England and Denmark, and
made an avenue typical of the most affectionate
welcome to the Princess Alexandra of Denmark, who, three days later, became Princess of
Wales.

Plenty of even quite young people can remember that holiday of general rejoicing when
the youthful and beautiful royal maiden entered
London in state, passing for miles between
serried masses of English people, who greeted
their own Prince and his chosen Bride in the
most loyal manner. Few who witnessed the
scene will ever forget it, and perhaps many a
student of history called to mind as he gazed,
incidents of the olden time when the Danes
came as conquerors of another sort—she to win

English hearts—they as conquerors fierce and
bold; but we may well forgive them—

> " For withal
> They dashed the salt spray in our face,
> And taught us 'neath their passing thrall,
> To win ourselves the Sea Kings' place ! "

The present London Bridge is a noble structure, massive and beautiful; its five elliptical
arches spanning the river in the most graceful
form. They afford such ample space for the rising
tide and rushing stream that navigation beneath
them is perfectly safe, which was not always the
case with the smaller arches of the old bridge.
Indeed the bridge which now adorns the City
of London, and takes its name from the metropolis just as its predecessor did, is a triumph of
engineering skill, well able to resist storm and
tempest, flood and frost, and is likely to endure
for uncounted centuries. May it ever be trod
by a Free People aspiring to virtue, and grateful for the blessings inherent in their Island
Home !

THE TEMPLE CHURCH.

HERE is scarcely an edifice in all England more full of historical associations than the Temple Church. Situated in the heart of the busiest metropolis in the world, and close to the river where the ships of all nations are moored, that beautiful church carries the mind back to remote ages. For it is by no mere figure of speech, but by following link by link a chain of circumstances, that we can trace events which connect it even with the Temple of Solomon. In our midst there still stands a memorial of the Crusades, and of the Knights

Templars who played so striking a part in mediæval history.

In these days laws and manners, and systems of government, are so different from what they were eight hundred years ago, that it requires a strong effort of the imagination to picture events in the guise in which at that period they really happened. History tells the sad story of wars and sieges all over the known world, but perhaps none are so deeply pathetic as the struggles which from time to time took place in Palestine, and the sieges to which Jerusalem was subjected.

The Bible relates those events which caused Palestine to be called the Holy Land, and after the Christian era its vicissitudes were many and great. The terrible siege of Jerusalem under Vespasian and Titus, A.D. 70, and its total destruction are well known; and in the following century the Romans built a heathen city on its site. But the old name was revived after the conversion to Christianity of the Emperor Constantine, who built a sacred edifice on the spot where the crucifixion of Our Saviour had taken place.

After being besieged by the Persians, and again falling into the hands of the Romans in the beginning of the seventh century, it was taken by the Saracens A.D. 637.

These people were Arabs newly converted to Mahommedanism. They had previously been an idolatrous race, worshipping the sun, moon and stars. The name Saracen—probably derived from an Arabic word signifying Eastern people—more especially belonged to the people dwelling between the Tigris and Euphrates, but in the course of time it became the name of all Arabs who had embraced the doctrines of Mahomet—and afterwards in the middle ages for all Mahommedans.

When the Saracens took Jerusalem Mahomet had only been dead six or seven years, and though from the first foundation of Mahommedanism there had always been great enmity between its followers and Christians, the feud had not as yet attained the rancour which afterwards distinguished it. Still it was a great blow to Christendom to feel that places made sacred by the sufferings of Our Lord were in

D

the hands of the Infidel; for pilgrimages to the
Holy Land were often made, so that besides the
sentiment of profanation which no doubt widely
prevailed, difficulties for pilgrims had to be
apprehended.

Before we can estimate what a pilgrimage
from France or England to the Holy Land really
meant in the early centuries of Christianity, we
must consider the difficulties of travelling
through long desolate tracts of country, or in
districts where crimes of violence were of frequent occurrence. No doubt many devout
persons undertook the long journey from merely
a strong religious impulse, but in numerous
instances it was performed as a penance enjoined
by the Romish Church for past sin, or as a
means of procuring what was called an indul-
gence.

The Saracens, however, permitted pilgrims to
visit the Holy Places, though they levied a capi-
tation tax for the privilege they awarded. And
the Caliph Haroun-Alraschid, who seems to have
been on friendly terms with the Emperor Charlemagne, sent to that monarch the keys of the

Holy Sepulchre as a free-will offering. This happened A.D. 801, and was looked on as a compliment to the Latin Church. But when in the eleventh century the Turks became masters of Jerusalem, a new era began, which was destined to influence many generations of men.

The Turks, though also Mahommedans, were far less refined than the Saracens, and far more cruel and rapacious. Not content with the tax which the Christians were willing to pay, these new masters of Jerusalem robbed and maltreated the pilgrims, treating them with the greatest cruelty and indignity. This conduct roused the spirit of the Christian nations, and in A.D. 1096 various expeditions were set on foot by men determined either to lay down their lives or to reach Jerusalem. The first body was led by a Burgundian named Gaultier, surnamed *Sans-avoir*, or as English writers call him Walter the Penniless, who apparently set out with the intention of begging his way to the Holy Land. It was a serious matter for the countries through which they had to pass, to feed and shelter a number of armed men who were little disciplined, and were rapacious from the urgency of their need. Thus we cannot wonder at the conflicts which took place.

Besides, the Turks—already powerful—resented any facilities offered to the pilgrims, and fanaticism on each side grew more and more violent. If, indeed, the pilgrims had been rich enough always to pay their way, and had carried much money about them, then probably they would have been waylaid and murdered for the sake of their gold, and perhaps not a man left to tell the story. For Europe was in a most lawless state, and might was honoured instead of right. The literal truth is, that these armed men set out with the determination of reaching Palestine at all hazards—of fighting their way whenever it was found necessary so to do.

This first body under Walter the Penniless was destroyed in Bulgaria. Then came the preaching of Peter the Hermit, and the expedition he himself led, which was likewise cut to pieces; a third, consisting mainly of German peasants, likewise perished; and the fourth, after committing dreadful atrocities and massacring the Jews in Mainz, were themselves well-nigh exterminated by the Hungarian army. It is very dreadful to reflect on the manner in which ignorant superstition and religious fanaticism were made the excuses for wholesale murder. No doubt it was the wealth of the Jews that caused their destruction. Debarred by the laws from all occupations except those of commerce, they devoted themselves energetically to trade, and in the middle ages were generally the wealthiest of citizens. Princes and Crusaders alike plundered the Jews, often on the shallowest pretexts.

The avowed object of the Crusaders, who fought under the banner of the Cross—hence their name—was to rescue Jerusalem from the Infidels; but by-and-by personal ambition mingled largely with their enterprises. Perhaps, however, the noblest and most pure-minded man who distinguished himself at this time was Godfrey de Bouillon. He was of noble birth, his father having been Count of Boulogne; while, through his mother, daughter of a Duke of Lorraine, he claimed descent from Charlemagne. In those

days men of his rank almost always devoted
themselves to military pursuits, and he was no
exception to the rule.   He became standard-
bearer in the army of the Emperor of Germany,
by whom he was made Marquis of Antwerp.
He had, however, to fight for the duchy of
Bouillon, which had been invaded in his absence, but after expelling the usurper he returned
to Germany and again distinguished himself in
connection with the Imperial army.

The story goes that while Godfrey was very
ill from a fever he heard of an expedition to
Jerusalem, and vowed that if he recovered his
health he would join in it.   An old chronicler
relates that directly he uttered this vow he
recovered his strength.   Soon afterwards he was
placed at the head of an immense army, estimated by some writers as more than a hundred
thousand men.   They were a motley concourse
divided into several bands, and many thousand
men never reached Palestine.   Godfrey, at the
head of one detachment—which when nearing
its destination was joined by some others—
pushed his way through Germany and Hungary,

and after many trials and losses arrived at Antioch, which town after a desperate resistance fell into the hands of the invaders June 3, 1098.

The Crusaders, however, were now in their turn attacked by a body of Persian Turks, whom they at last defeated, mainly it was said by the enthusiasm that was kindled by a French priest who believed that he had had an encouraging vision of St. Andrew. The Crusaders had suffered terribly from famine and pestilence, but such as remained fit for the expedition marched on to Jerusalem, where they arrived in 1099.

Now began that terrible siege which lasted five weeks, during which the most horrible sufferings were inflicted and endured by both parties. Several chiefs besides Godfrey greatly distinguished themselves, conspicuous among them having been Tancred, and Robert Duke of Normandy, eldest son of William the Conquerer. These two Princes were those who forced one of the gates, and may be said to have planted the standard of the Cross on the walls of Jerusalem.

You must bear in mind that the fighting was
chiefly carried on by means of cross-bows and
arrows—for gunpowder was not yet invented—
and movable towers, which protected the men
inside them. But the Turks, well acquainted
with what was called Greek fire, poured out
flame upon their assailants. No doubt the fury
of the struggle roused the fiercest passions on
both sides; but it is sad to think, and sad to
tell, of the cruelties which were perpetrated by
men who professed Christianity and fought
under the banner of the Cross. The Turks
unable to resist their enemies fled in numbers to
the Mosques, and were slain there without
distinction of age or condition ; while those in
the streets and houses, even the women and
children, were massacred by thousands. The
streets literally flowed with human blood.

The Crusaders justified themselves for their
vengeance, by believing it a deserved retribution
on the Infidel for his oppression of Christians.
It is probable, indeed, that they thought the
extermination of the Turks a duty laid upon
them, so little at that time was the teaching of

Our Lord understood, or his command to forgive injuries acted on.

Now that Jerusalem was conquered it became necessary to place it in the hands of some powerful prince, and Godfrey was duly elected the first King of Jerusalem. He was solemnly invested with this new dignity in the Church of the Holy Sepulchre, but would not allow himself to be crowned, saying it was not fit that he should wear a diadem of gold in the city where his Saviour had been crowned with thorns. He indeed only called himself "Defender and Baron of the Holy Sepulchre." After the capture of Jerusalem, Godfrey gained further possessions in the East, all of which consolidated his power, but he only lived a year, dying July 17th, 1100. For many centuries his tomb was an object of devout interest, and his sword is still preserved at Jerusalem as a precious relic. In Brussels there is a very fine equestrian statue of Godfrey de Bouillon holding aloft the standard; and this hero of the Crusaders is immortalized in Tasso's great poem of "Jerusalem Delivered."

Though Godfrey's reign was so short he had

instituted a wise code of laws for his subjects. He was succeeded by his brother Baldwin, who reigned till 1118 under the title of Baldwin the First. On his death, after many conflicts with the Saracens, his cousin became King of Jerusalem as Baldwin the Second. This prince, unlike Godfrey, consented to be crowned and the ceremony was performed with great solemnity. " They put the ring on his finger as signifying faith; then they girded on the sword which means justice, to defend the faith and holy Church; and after that the crown which signifies dignity; and then the sceptre which signifies to defend and punish; and then the apple or globe which signifies the earth and soil of the kingdom."

Baldwin the Second was often in conflict with the Saracens, but though he was taken prisoner and had many changes of fortune, he left the kingdom of Jerusalem greatly enlarged. It was during his reign that the Pope sanctioned the institution of the Knights of St. John of Jerusalem, and of the Knights Templars.

Though the little kingdom of Jerusalem was

certainly established to the great joy of all
Christendom, the Mahommedans never relin-
quished the idea of regaining their possessions.
Consequently it was found necessary to be constantly prepared to repel attacks. The Turks
were still powerful enough to be dreaded if
vigilance were once relaxed, and the standing
difficulties of pilgrims in travelling great dis-
tances still remained. It was for the protection
of pilgrims that the two famous orders of
knighthood were originally instituted.

The Knights Hospitallers of St. John devoted
themselves to providing hospitality for pilgrims,
according to their first vow, though they were
also warriors who fought against the Infidels.

The Knights Templars were a fraternity of a
somewhat similar order, but for a time were a
more powerful one. They took their name from
the circumstance that Baldwin the Second gave
them apartments on Mount Moriah, within the
enclosure of the Temple of Jerusalem, whence
they were speedily called Knights of the Temple
of Solomon, and afterwards Knights Templars.

About A.D. 1119, nine French gentlemen

formed themselves into a body for the avowed
purpose of defending pilgrims on their way to
the Holy Land.   These knights, though of
gentle birth, are believed to have been very poor,
but their wealth and their numbers soon
increased; they were organized into a society
with a Grand Master and a distinguishing dress.
This was a white mantle, with a red cross upon
it.   In battle they displayed a black and white
banner, inscribed "Non nobis Domine, non nobis,
sed nomini tuo da gloriam,"   Not unto us, O
Lord, not unto us, but unto Thy Name give
the praise.   Either to symbolize their original
poverty or commemorate a fact, they adopted for
the seal of their Order the device of two men
riding on one horse.

In the twelfth century news did not travel
very fast.   Tidings from the Holy Land, however,
were always full of interest, and travellers on
their return home were eagerly welcomed.   The
pilgrim generally wore a cockle shell in his hat
of a sort found on the Syrian shore, with a
wallet slung on his shoulders, and had a staff in
his hand; and the appearance of one of these

personages was enough to ensure hospitality among honest folks. This he requited by relating his own adventures, and telling of the deeds performed and dangers encountered by others. Often the pilgrim had his staff wreathed with palm-leaves gathered in Palestine, and which he carried as proof that he had really been there. Hence he was sometimes called a "palmer."

It was from returned pilgrims no doubt that the English first heard of the Knights Templars, and were in some measure prepared for a party of them which arrived in England A.D. 1128. Hugh de Payens, one of the first nine knights who founded the Order, was now Grand Master; and selecting four of the brethren for his companions he journeyed from Jerusalem to our shores, for the express purpose of explaining to Henry the First and his nobility the objects of the Society of Templars.

So successful was he that after his visit to England he returned to Jerusalem with three hundred fresh brethren belonging to the noblest families, mainly those of England and France.

There was something very attractive to the
mediæval mind in the combination of warlike
fame and religious holiness; and no doubt many
of the Templars in the early days of the Order
were men who sincerely desired to devote themselves to the service of God.   They vowed
individual poverty, obedience to their superiors, and not to marry.   But as wealth flowed
in to the common stock many temptations
sprang up.   They affiliated " serving brothers"
to attend upon them from the citizen class which
they despised, and their Grand Master was
allowed to hold the rank of a prince.   They were
in truth very powerful, and their pride and
arrogance became proverbial.

Before Hugh de Payens left England he
established a society in this country, with a
Knight called a " Prior of the Temple" at the
head of it to manage the affairs of the Order
and transmit the money accumulated to Jerusalem.   Many establishments connected with
the order now sprang up in the country, the
principal one being in London, in Holborn, on
the spot where Southampton Buildings at pre-

sent stand. This house Hugh de Payens himself saw established.

But in fifty years the English Templars were greatly increased in numbers, and they wanted more magnificent buildings than they as yet possessed. They had wealth to gratify their wishes, and purchased a site which was probably then one of the most delightful in London—namely the ground on which the Temple Church, the Temple Gardens, and those Inns of Court called Inner and Middle Temple now stand. In the old times " Inn " meant place of residence —not merely a temporary abode. On this spot they began erecting a beautiful church on the model of the Holy Sepulchre at Jerusalem, and extensive adjacent buildings for the accommodation of the Order.

Some time, however, before the works were completed, great troubles fell upon their brethren in Palestine in consequence of the increasing power of the Saracens, who after Saladin became their leader vanquished the Christian armies on several occasions. These misfortunes brought Heraclius the Patriarch of Jerusalem to England, accompanied by the Master of St. John's. The Master of the Temple had also set out, but he had died on the way.

The object of these illustrious visitors was a personal interview with the English king, Henry the Second, to enlist his sympathies and obtain promises of assistance. Henry received them very graciously and appeared much moved by their description of affairs in Palestine, and the great risk there was of the Holy Land again passing into the power of the Infidel. Indeed they had some claim on the ,'s considera- tion, for on obtaining abso ι for his par- ticipation in the murder of Thomas à Becket he had promised to lead an army to Palestine, and to maintain at his own charge a certain number of Templars. But the only assurance that Henry could now give was a promise to consult the Parliament directly it met.

Meanwhile—it was A.D. 1185—the English Templars took advantage of the arrival of the Patriarch, to solicit from him a great honour; namely that he should consecrate and open with all due ceremonies their new home. This

TEMPLE CHURCH.

he gladly consented to do; and, familiar as he was with oriental magnificence, there is little doubt that he was both surprised and delighted at the architectural beauties he beheld. The Templars were already rich, and they had lavished their wealth on the buildings now just finished. It was an age when workmen were plentiful and laborious, and when the designs of the architect were carried out with patience, good faith, and skill. The church, with its circular colonnade and tesselated pavement, its stained glass windows and decorated ceiling, was almost unique in form, and would alone have proved the resources of the Order.

But in harmony with the Church were the quiet cloisters, the separate homes for the Prior, the chaplains, and the Knights, as well as for the inferior serving brothers, and all sorts of domestics. There were the Chapter-house where they met to transact business, and the spacious Refectory where they dined, with all sorts of needful offices. A beautiful garden sloped down to the Thames—and here the Knights practised military exercises and trained their horses.

E

No doubt Heraclius was delighted with the prosperity of the English Templars; but the Knights of St. John were also growing rich, and were highly esteemed, and the Patriarch consecrated their church in Clerkenwell likewise. It is sad to say, that within the next century the rivalry of these two noble Orders became so extreme that, instead of co-operating for the good of Christendom, they grew into bitter, remorseless enemies.

The Patriarch was doomed to a grave disappointment with regard to obtaining assistance from the King.

It is only fair to admit that Henry's position was trying. Whether he really wished to fulfil his vow or not, it is impossible to say; he professed to do so, but when Parliament met the Barons declared that by his coronation oath he was bound to stay in England and govern the realm. Something of a compromise was attempted, and an offer was made to raise money for the expenses of a body of troops, to be commanded by such nobles and others as desired to join the Christian warriors. Lastly, the King offered "to give largely of his own" to such "as would undertake the voyage," though he could not leave his country to be the prey of Frenchmen.

This answer aroused the wrath and indignation of the Patriarch, who replied with bitterness,—

"We seek a man, and not money; well-near every Christian region sendeth unto us money, but no land sendeth to us a Prince. Therefore, we ask a Prince that needeth money, and not money that needeth a Prince."

But the King still made excuses, and the Patriarch "departed from him discontented and comfortless, whereof the King being advertised, intending somewhat to recomfort him with pleasant words, followed him unto the sea-side." So little effect, however, had Henry's "pleasant words" that Heraclius broke out into still more violent speech, exclaiming, after fresh reproaches, "Do by me right as thou didst by that blessed man Thomas of Canterbury, for I had liever be slain by thee than of the Saracens, for thou art worse than any Saracen."

The King, still keeping his temper, replied,

E 2

"I may not wend out of my land, for my own sons will arise against me when I was absent."

"No wonder," replied the Patriarch, "for of the Devil they come, and to the Devil they shall go," and then departed from the King in great wrath.

Henry appears to have borne meekly these insulting taunts. Perhaps after the penance and humilation to which he had submitted, in consequence of the murder of Becket, at his supposed instigation, he felt that he could endure anything from a dignitary of the Church. Those who remember the history of Henry's son, Richard Cœur de Lion, know that the Christians in Palestine did get a Prince to fight for them.

The consecration of their new church, and the occupation of the adjacent and commodious building by the Templars, formed a memorable era in the history of the Order. Now it seemed firmly established in England. The head of the house was called Master of the Temple—the supreme head at Jerusalem being entitled Grand Master.

The jurisdiction of the Master of the Temple extended not only over his own house in London, but over all the priors or preceptors of provincial establishments. He was elected in an assembly of Knights from one of themselves, and no doubt the position was coveted eagerly by those who were ambitious of power. But to be simply a brother of the Order was itself a title of honour.

The installation of the Knights was a very solemn and religious ceremony, which it is supposed took place in a chapel on the south-side of the Round of the Church, which chapel existed till the year 1827. The candidate—who had previously been examined and questioned—appeared before the assembly of Knights, when with folded hands and kneeling before the Master he humbly entreated to be received into the Order—to share in its good deeds, and to be through life its slave and servant.

Then the Master represented to him what a "great matter" he was asking, saying to him that he only saw the outward shell of the Order —how that the Knights were splendidly dressed and had fine horses richly caparisoned; that they fared sumptuously with regard to meat and drink; but that he knew not yet all the hardships he should have to encounter. He reminded him how his own will must in all things give way under his vow of obedience — how when he wanted to sleep he might be ordered to watch; how when he wanted to eat he might be ordered to do something else ; and many other certain trials were pointed out to him. Consenting to everything the candidate was at last received and assured of " bread and water, and the poor clothing of the Order, and labour and toil enow." Then the famous white mantle with the red cross on the shoulder, was placed upon him by the Master, who kissed him, as did the chaplain.

This ceremony completed, the Master delivered a discourse enumerating the duties of the Knights Templars—or Red Cross Knights, as they were sometimes called. They were commanded never to strike or maltreat any Christian ; never to swear ; never to receive attendance from a woman without permission ; never to abuse or call names, but on all occasions to be courteous and polite. As women often attended wounded warriors, dressing their wounds and ministering to them, possibly the order relating to women was intended in some measure to prevent these soldiers of the Cross growing effeminate by accepting services when not absolutely necessary.

The Knight was ordered to perform certain duties with regularity, such as attending divine service, and never to sit down to table or rise from it without prayer. He was to sleep in his hose and with a girdle round his waist— no doubt that he might be promptly ready for any duty demanded of him. He was also to recite a certain number of *pater nosters* when the Master died.

The Master's exhortation over, the newly received brother was presented with clothes, and all necessary arms and equipments, and henceforth he was to appear only arrayed as a Knight Templar. He was generally given three horses, and allowed an esquire—sometimes a youth of noble birth—to attend upon him.

The rules of the Order must have pressed very differently upon different characters. No doubt it numbered among its members many earnest men, who honestly believed that the cause of Christianity could be best served by extirpating the Infidel. There is no record of their having tried gentle measures of persuasion, and of having shown the beauty of holiness, and the superiority of their own faith by deeds of loving kindness. Indeed, there is good reason to believe that the Saracens were often their superiors in courtesy and generosity.

Some Templars, perhaps, cared less for the spread of Christianity than for their individual glory and renown; some, perhaps, knowing their own frailties, put themselves in subjection as a means of discipline. However this may have been, the Order generally increased in riches and dignity. But when, notwithstanding the efforts of Richard Cœur de Lion and his fellow-crusaders, Palestine again fell into the hands of the Infidel, the establishment of the Knights Templars in Jerusalem was broken up, and after some vicissitudes they established their head-quarters in France. By this time they numbered many thousands, and for a while they still continued to grow in wealth and fame.

But, perhaps, in the same way that the riches . of the Jews in the middle ages brought persecution and robbery on them, so the vast possessions of the Knights Templars set needy princes coveting their treasures. Being human, the Templars were no doubt often faulty, and they held so prominent a place in the world, that something of "the fierce light which beats upon a throne" beat also upon them, to reveal their frailties, and often in an exaggerated manner. But that they were guilty of the atrocious crimes their enemies imputed to them, few students of history can believe. The real truth seems to be that unscrupulous princes wanted their wealth, and miserable wretches were found to act the part of false witnesses, and plot their ruin.

Yet it was not till the reign of Edward II. that the overthrow of the unfortunate Templars was effected. Philip of France, the Pope, and the weak English King were equally greedy of the riches possessed by the Knights, and equally determined to break up the Order. Let us hope that these potentates at least believed some of the accusations made against the Templars. Even then their cruelty was monstrous.

It was the age when frightful tortures were inflicted on criminals with the avowed object of leading them to confess the crimes of which they were accused. Multitudes of miserable innocent people, unable to bear their torments, have said whatever their accusers demanded, desiring only a speedy death to end their sufferings. This was the case with the Grand Master James de Molay and three other Templars. But, contrary to expectation, De Molay, when called upon to repeat his confession in public in Paris, on a scaffold in front of the church of Notre Dame, instead of doing so, raised his chained hands and solemnly recanted it.

"I acknowledge," he said, "though to my eternal shame, that I have committed the greatest of crimes; but it has been the acknowledging of those which have been so foully charged on the Order. I attest, and truth obliges me to attest, that it is innocent. I made the contrary declaration only to suspend the excessive pains of torture, and to mollify those who made me

endure them. I know the punishments which
have been inflicted on all the Knights who had
the courage to revoke a similar confession; but
the dreadful spectacle which is presented to me
is not able to make me confirm one lie by another."

One of the other Templars followed the great
example of his Master. Both were burnt to
death by slow fire that same evening.

Meanwhile the order in England had been
treated with nearly equal severity. For a time,
it is true, Edward the Second had professed to
be their friend and protector, but a papal bull or
decree of the Pope seems suddenly to have
changed his opinions. For a little while Edward
was opposed to torture being inflicted, but after
some demur, he yielded, and gave up the Templars to the power of the papal inquisitors.

When first interrogated every Knight, without
exception, maintained the innocence of the Order;
but torture was applied, and a chaplain and
two serving men made the desired statement—
confession it was called—as to the Order's denial
of the Saviour. On this as individuals they were

pardoned. But the other Templars were bravely resolute. At last they were brought to acknowledge that they had believed the Master had the power of absolution. This was declared to be rank heresy—and sufficient excuse to despoil them of their wealth. They were required to make a public confession of their fault, and on doing so were re-admitted to the Christian community. But they were utterly beggared, and many of them must have starved had not some of the chief ecclesiastics had compassion on them and procured their admission into religious houses.

Nominally the property of the Order was transferred to the rival Order of St. John of Jerusalem, the Knights Hospitallers, now established in the island of Rhodes and called Knights of Rhodes. But they did not enter on their inheritance without great limitations. The kings of France and England as well as some other princes shared in the spoils, and the Pope probably claimed precisely what he pleased.

It would have been very difficult for the

Knights of Rhodes to establish their full claim
to the English property against the will of the
English king, and probably they took a course
as wise as generous in demising the church,
gardens, and stately buildings belonging to the
London Templars, with " all the appurtenances,"
to certain students of the common law. This
event took place in the twentieth year of the
reign of Edward the Third, and ever since then
the home and the haunt of the English Knights
Templars has been devoted to the study and
practice of the law.

Whatever hold the Knights of Rhodes might
retain over the property ceased at the time of
the Reformation, when Henry the Eighth suppressed all monastic orders, doing just what he
pleased with their funds. After this period the
Inns of Court were held by lease from the
Crown.

The Knights Hospitallers retained the island
of Rhodes for more than two hundred years,
increasing in fame and opulence. Gibbon the
historian speaks of them as a " bulwark of
Christendom " that " provoked and repelled the

arms of the Turks and Saracens." It was still considered their prime duty to exterminate the Infidel if possible, and they lost no opportunity of attacking their enemies. It was their habit in their island home to keep perpetual watch for Saracen ships. Woe betide a solitary vessel that steered within sight—the Knights immediately sent out a little fleet to chase and capture it. We find it difficult to look upon such conduct as anything but cruel piracy—yet the Knights held themselves to be perpetually at war with the Infidel and extenuated their actions accordingly.

In 1522, however, they were overcome by the Turks, and had to surrender Rhodes. For a few years they were without a permanent home, till in 1530 Charles the Fifth bestowed the Island of Malta, with some other territory upon them, and henceforth they were called Knights of Malta. But the world was gradually changing, and though the body of Knights known by so many different names still remained sometimes to do good service in many sorts of ways, its power in time decayed. In 1798 Napoleon the First seized Malta, and soon afterwards the Order was dispersed.

When we read history with intelligence and sympathy we feel how mysteriously past and present—old things and new—are linked together. Though the main buildings of the Knights Templars in London may have yielded to fire and time, and to the changes necessary for a change of purposes, the beautiful Church still remains, restored in a reverent spirit within the last few years, so that the visitor or worshipper feels that he is indeed standing or kneeling where, with little change, the monastic warriors prayed and preached and did penance centuries ago.

How different was their mode of life from anything experienced to-day ! The poorest classes of people now enjoy comforts and luxuries to which the magnificent Knights Templars were wholly strangers. Not a printed book existed, and there were very few writings in the world except copies of the Scriptures in Latin and Greek. These manuscripts were often rightly judged more precious than their weight in gold. Reading was thought a great accomplishment, and to be able to write something extraordinary. We may be pretty sure that except the Chaplains, and probably the Masters, few of the Knights Templars could either read or write with anything like facility.

Then in the matter of their diet—how limited it was! Tea and coffee and potatoes and the greater number of our fruits and vegetables were wholly unknown to them. Wine was sold in small quantities as a cordial, and was probably looked on as a medicine; though it is likely enough that those Templars who had travelled in the East had tasted the Greek wines and perhaps some others. However, they had the best of all beverages close at hand, their fountain of pure water in the Temple Gardens, and the bright river called for many generations after their day the Silver Thames.

The river swarmed with fish, so that no doubt they had fresh delicious fare for their so-called fast-days; and we may be sure that country friends supplied them with venison and other

game very often, and we know they had plenty
of money to purchase anything in the market.
But it was a strange life, without reading and
without postal communication, and we can
fancy how the Templars told travellers' tales
over and over again for want of novelties to
think about. Sun-dials and hour-glasses must
have been used by them instead of clocks.

In the Temple Church are several effigies of
Knights remaining, those which have the legs
crossed commemorating Brothers of the Order
who had travelled to the Holy Land. This
attitude in old monuments always indicates a
Crusader.

But though the Knights Templars knew how
to honour their Order, they also knew very well
how to punish refractory members of it. There
is still to be seen at the side of the Church the
penitential cell in which culprits were confined,
often for long periods. It is reached by a narrow
staircase, and measures less than five feet in
length by two and a half in breath, so that a
well grown man could not lie down at full
length in it. There were apertures, however,

F

looking into the Church through which he could hear the service. This appeared as if the Order had care for the souls of their erring brothers, however cruelly their bodies were treated. In this wretched cell the Grand Preceptor of Ireland was fettered by command of the Master, and died in his misery. At daybreak his body was ignominiously buried between the Church and the Hall.

Sometimes, for what we should call trivial offences, the Knights were publicly scourged. One of them quitted the Order, but either impelled by superstitious terrors or really repentant of his faults, he voluntarily returned and submitted himself to whatever penance the Master chose to inflict. He was condemned to fast on bread and water four days in the week, and to eat with the dogs on the ground for a year, and to be scourged in the church every Sunday.

Of course this severity of discipline, and the courage and piety of those who submitted to it, had great weight with the outer world in days when true religion was mingled with much superstition, and the brave endurance of severe penance was thought admirable in the extreme. It became an object of ambition to be buried among the Knights Templars, and the noble and the rich often showered wealth on the Order, for the purpose of purchasing the privilege they so much coveted. Sometimes great people in trouble took refuge with the Templars and were hospitably entertained by them, notably King John, who dated many documents from the Temple.

They also knew how to be kind and generous to the miserable on occasion. There was a baron Geoffrey de Magnaville, son of one of the same name who fought at Hastings, who, for many sins, had been excommunicated by the Church. The Templars, however, believing him penitent, had enrolled him among their Order. But when he died they dared not bury him in consecrated ground, so hung up his corpse in a leaden coffin on a tree in the garden, until after some years they obtained absolution for him, and buried him near the western door. No doubt his grave clothes were of sack-cloth, like those of many less

erring brothers.   His effigy is still to be seen in
the Church.

Much wealth was sometimes confided to the
safe keeping of the Templars, and perhaps from
various circumstances of those unsettled times it
was often not reclaimed.   When Edward the
First returned from the conquest of Wales he
professed a great desire to see his mother's
jewels, which had been placed in charge of the
Templars.   He was admitted, and carried off
ten thousand pounds, as the Templars declared,
by breaking . open their coffers.   It was not
possible to resist a King ; and by this time they
were looked on as little wanted for anything except their money.

But they had made their immortal mark on
the pages of mediæval history.   We cannot read
of Europe in the twelfth and thirteenth centuries
without perceiving what an influence the Order
of Knights Templars exercised, and speculating
on the characters of the men who composed it.
Great qualities were required to fulfil worthily
many difficult duties.   Pride in the Order, which
made every brother desire to uphold its dignity,

was often combined with the extreme of personal humility. Undauntable courage was allied to unquestioning obedience to the Master, and the power of ready self-denial was exacted from men of lineage trained to command. It is impossible to think of the Knights Templars and their romantic history without feeling that the London district which is called the Temple is hallowed ground.

THE ROYAL EXCHANGE.

THE Royal Exchange is one of the City sights which foreigners and country cousins visiting the Metropolis generally desire to see; though perhaps some people living at the other end of London know little more about it than the strangers whose curiosity has been aroused by their recollections of history. The Royal Exchange, however, is not only intimately associated with English history, but with the biography of a very remarkable man.

Sir Thomas Gresham was born in 1519, in those early days of Henry the Eighth's reign, when the King had shown none of the vices

which made him abhorred in later years. The
Greshams were a Norfolk family, who, for several
generations, had been people of wealth and influence and good repute. The father and two of
the uncles of the famous Thomas were eminent
and prosperous merchants, and from his earliest
years he himself was intended for a mercantile
career. Nevertheless, like a wise man, his
father, Sir Richard, bestowed a liberal education
on him at one of the Universities, and we are
quite justified in looking at the future mercer
and merchant as a scholar and finished gentleman. Indeed, without advantages of learning
and courtly manners he would have been little
likely to become the counsellor and trusted emis-
sary of princes.

In reading about London in the middle ages
we often come upon the terms Mercer and Merchant-adventurer. Mercer, which now means
a dealer in silks and woollen cloths, in remote
times was the term applied to a dealer in various
small wares ; but as the commerce of England
developed the Mercers became more and more
important, until mercer and merchant were

words used with almost the same meaning. The Mercers' Company, incorporated in the fourteenth century, ranks first of all the City Companies, and has enrolled among its members many royal and noble personages. Nearly a hundred Lord Mayors have been elected from it, and perhaps more than any other body it is associated with the commerce of London.

There can be little doubt that Thomas Gresham early in life showed abilities far above the common average; but throughout his whole career these natural talents were aided by great energy of character and a degree of shrewdness and prudence in worldly affairs that have seldom been surpassed. So early as at the age of twenty-four he was a merchant of repute, and before he was thirty-two he became what was called King's Merchant or Factor, and was entrusted with the management of affairs of the greatest importance.

Kings of England, and especially the Tudor sovereigns, were often very much in want of money. Hard and unjust laws prevented the natural wealth of the country from being developed, while frequent wars and lavish gifts to favourites helped to exhaust the treasury. In the time of Henry the Eighth and his immediate successors, Antwerp was the great emporium of commerce, and being consequently probably the richest city in the world, its merchants became the greatest of money lenders. Now, the Tudor sovereigns were great borrowers, and they so often wanted money, and I am sorry to say were for the most part such bad paymasters, that the rich Antwerp merchants always bargained for enormous interest—as much sometimes as fourteen per cent. or perhaps even more; and not content with this sort of extortion they very frequently insisted on jewels being taken in part instead of money. They knew exceedingly well the real value of precious stones, and we may be pretty sure they put the very highest price on those of which they so disposed.

Gresham married when he was about five or six and twenty, and had a son born before he became King's Factor. During the years when he had only been what was called a Merchant-adventurer his business had frequently taken

him to Antwerp, and no doubt he had made
acquaintance with the rich merchants and
money lenders of that City; thus he was in all
respects well qualified to be entrusted with
Government affairs. Gresham had not only to
negotiate loans, but to purchase ammunition,
and to report all sorts of desirable information
to the Privy Council.

There is a proverb that "birds of a feather
flock together," and it is a very true one; for it
is generally a fair test of any one to judge him
by the character of his intimate friends and
associates. It was necessary that Gresham
should have a home at Antwerp, and with his
wife and family he was allowed to take up his
abode with a very eminent man. This was
Jasper Schetz, the eldest of three brothers whose
firm was one with the highest reputation of any
in Antwerp, and whose unanimity was so remarkable that a medal with their names and
armorial bearings was struck to commemorate it.
All were distinguished men, but Jasper was the
most important of the brothers. He was a
scholar and poet as well as a man of business,

and was employed by the Emperor Charles the
Fifth in the same office that Gresham filled for
the English King. As Gresham speaks of Jasper
Schetz as his "very friend" we may infer that
they had the most congenial tastes and opinions.

Gresham however did not live with any regularity at Antwerp; he made frequent journeys
to London, partly no doubt on his own affairs,
in the conduct of which he had to employ
agents, but often because he was sent for by the
young King. Indeed it is said that in the two
first years of Edward the Sixth's reign he
journeyed from Antwerp to the Court no less
than forty times. When we remember how
comparatively slow travelling was in those days,
it seems as if Gresham must have spent more
time on the road and on the sea than in his own
home. Before the days of steam navigation the
sea passage must often have been tedious, and
always uncertain, depending as it did on the
wind and the weather; and as for the land travelling coaches were only just coming into use,
and men almost always made journeys on horseback.

When the boy-king Edward the Sixth died, and Mary came to the throne, Gresham was hastily dismissed. He was known to be a staunch protestant, and only papists seemed now to have a chance of court favour. He had, however, a very warm friend in Sir John à Leye, or Leigh, whose acquaintance he had probably made abroad, and who interceded for him, and evidently made some impression on the Queen and her ministers. But Gresham himself wrote to Queen Mary, enumerating his services, and explaining how by his good management he had discharged the late King's debts, which otherwise would have embarrassed her Majesty. There is no doubt Gresham was a most efficient agent, and moreover it was always his policy to persuade the English Government to pay its debts punctually according to promise, by which means he was an instrument to improve its credit and obtain money on the most favourable terms.

Nothwithstanding the hot bigotry of Mary and her persecution of protestants, Gresham returned to Antwerp and resumed his office in connection with the English Government, only a few months after Queen Mary's accession; a circumstance, I think, conclusive that no Roman Catholic equally competent for his duties could be found to supersede him. Mary wanted money quite as much as her father and brother had done, and Gresham had many arduous tasks during her reign.

His position, indeed, was a very difficult one. There is really no reason to believe that he in any way conformed to the Romish faith, though it is likely enough that he did not give speech to his protestant convictions during the five years of Mary's reign. As long as he fulfilled his duties as the Queen's agent, and kept a quiet tongue with regard to his religious opinions, he seems to have suffered no farther inconvenience than that of making a great many enemies among the bigots of the time, many of whom, no doubt, were envious of his influential position and growing wealth. For Gresham received a percentage on the loans he negotiated, and though he often complained of being badly paid, he early in life began to accumulate a fortune.

Perhaps, however, the accession of Queen

Elizabeth should be considered the great turning point in Gresham's career. This event took place on the 17th November, 1558. During the preceding summer, Gresham had been in England, but it is known that he returned to the continent in October. He must, however, have been again on his way to London, when the news of Queen Mary's death reached him, or in those days of slow travelling he could not have received the intelligence and started so as to arrive by the 20th, on which day he was one of a group of statesmen who had audience of the new Queen.

At this period Gresham was in his fortieth year, in the full vigour of his intellectual faculties, and with a vast fund of experience in dealing with men and state affairs. From the portraits which remain of him there is no doubt he was a man of a striking presence, and something above the average height, though unfortunately lame. There is a well known portrait of him by Sir Anthony More, a celebrated painter, who, in fact, painted him several times, and was probably his intimate friend.

The portrait, however, in question, and which is the most familiar to people through engravings, represents him in sober costume and wearing a black cap on his head. In his left hand he holds a small object which looks like an orange, but is really intended for a pomander, the name given to a ball of spices and perfumes, which was thought to be a safeguard against infection. Sometimes a pomander was really made of a dried Seville orange filled with cloves and other spices. There was a sort of fashion in using these scented balls, and they are often to be noticed in old portraits either hanging from the girdle or held in the hand. It is to be observed that the hand which holds the pomander also wears a ring, which, like gloves, in a portrait of the sixteenth century, may always be trusted as a sign of social distinction. In the middle ages, there was a marked difference of dress among different classes, and for a long time what were called sumptuary laws prevailed, which regulated the attire of different orders of society.

Elizabeth was staying at Hatfield when the

news of her sister's death reached her, and she found herself acknowledged as Queen of England; and certainly that first council of hers, at which Gresham was present, and Sir William Cecil was appointed Secretary of State, deserves to be remembered as an epoch in English History. Elizabeth, now five-and-twenty years of age, was in the bloom of her beauty, but she had led a life of great retirement, and had known a period of imprisonment. She had long been the hope of the Protestant party and she was soon to be its idol. She had been highly educated, and was what even now would be called a learned lady; but the most striking characteristic of the great Queen was her shrewd judgment, her power of penetrating beneath false appearances and discovering the real qualities of the people about her, and their fitness for different employments.

Cecil was Gresham's friend, and it is highly probable that he may have spoken of him favourably to Elizabeth. However this may have been, Gresham was at once reinstated as the Queen's Factor. Years afterwards he wrote of the Queen's reception of him, and of her graciously saying that "on the faith of a queen" she would "keep one ear shut to hear him," evidently meaning that she would not believe any evil report of his enemies, but always hold an ear closed from them to listen to his defence. Also she said that "if he did her no other service then he had done for her late brother King Edward and her late sister Queen Mary she would give him as much land as ever they both did." So you see when Gresham started afresh on his career under Queen Elizabeth he did so under the most favourable auspices, and early in December we find him again at Antwerp. Previously, however, he seems to have addressed a remarkable letter to the new Queen, a letter in which he expounded his views on financial affairs, and which was possibly written at a request from her that he should express his opinions in writing. It is full of good advice, and dwells strongly on the necessity of keeping up her credit by just and punctual payments, especially to her own merchants, on whom she would have to rely. I

G

wish, though, he had not emphasized this duty
to her own people as of more account than to
foreigners.

All along Gresham advocated borrowing from
London merchants whenever it was possible,
instead of from foreigners, that the interest
required might not go out of the country; but
many preceding monarchs had been such
extortioners, and dishonourable debtors, that
their own people were often unwilling to help
them even when able to do so.   To Gresham the
nation was largely indebted for bringing about
a better state of things, and there is abundant
evidence that Elizabeth heartly approved of his
views and valued his services.   In the year after
her accession she conferred on him the honour
of knighthood and appointed him temporary
ambassador at the Netherlands; and it may be
observed that about this time he had the
opportunity of showing his gratitude to Sir
John Leigh, who appears to have been in some
political difficulty now that so many Roman
Catholics lay under suspicion of disloyalty.
Writing to Sir William Cecil, Gresham pleads

for his friend, saying, " verily, Sir, it was the man that preserved me when Queen Mary came to the crown, for the which I do account myself bound to him during my life."

The next few years were probably the happiest of Gresham's life, but in 1564 he lost his only son, whom he had looked on as the inheritor of his fortune and in some sort of his honours. It was soon after this sad event that he projected the scheme of the Exchange, and it has been thought that if his son had lived he might not have exercised so much generosity as he subsequently did.

Gresham had long lamented that while the merchants of Antwerp had a spacious and commodious covered Bourse, where they could assemble to negotiate their business, Englishmen had to meet for the purpose in the open street. Indeed, his father, Sir Richard, had projected some suitable erection more than twenty years previously; so that although the death of Gresham's son might have stimulated the zeal of the bereaved father, and made him more promptly lavish in his generosity, the idea of

the Exchange could have been nothing new to
him.

"On 'Change!" What a common phrase it is
to describe a meeting-place for the transaction
of business! Of course, in a commercial city it
is necessary that there should be an established
resort, where, at a certain hour, certain persons
may be met; where, if one man wants to charter
a ship, and a ship-owner has a vessel that will
suit him, the bargain may be struck; where
contracts for various sorts of merchandise may
be made; and where Bills of Exchange, as re-
presentatives of money, may be bought or sold.
"On 'Change," also, prices are discussed, and
commercial news circulates. The Exchange is,
in fact, a focus of mercantile life wherever it
exists, and notably so in the City of London.

There can be little doubt that Gresham was
one of the wealthiest of citizens. He had two
or three country mansions of great splendour,
and a town house in Lombard Street, where his
business was transacted. Subsequently he had
a magnificent house in Bishopsgate Street. In
Queen Elizabeth's time many mansions of the

nobility and wealthy people were in that part
of London, now wholly devoted to counting-
houses, shops and warehouses. Indeed, what
is now called the West-end was then quite
country. The Strand, which had watercourses
covered with bridges running through it, had
splendid buildings, with terraces and gardens on
the banks of the Thames. These were the
residences of the nobility, who always had their
own barges, in which they were rowed from
place to place by servants in gorgeous liveries—
so that it was convenient to have steps from
their own gardens leading to the river. Only
about the time of Edward VI. were houses
built on the opposite or north side of the road;
and these houses are described as having beautiful gardens also, with numerous apple-trees in
them, stretching towards meadow-land, where
cattle grazed and milkmaids had much employment. It was open country beyond, and the
view extended to the hills of Highgate and
Hampstead. Fancy what a picturesque London
it must have been in those days!

The names of several streets branching off

from the Strand, such as Norfolk, Essex, Salisbury, Buckingham, and others, remind us of far different times and manners, when noblemen bearing those titles had princely dwellings near the river, which was a highway from one part of London to another, and also to a number of country places on its banks. Many of these beautiful districts are still favourite resorts; only times are altered, and we go to them now by railway or steamboat. Yet many of the old houses and old trees that we pass, if they could but think and talk, might tell us stories of the old days through which they have existed, and the generations they have survived.

Gresham's town house, however, was not near the river, though it probably rivalled in magnificence the great houses at the Strand. It was in his mansion in Bishopsgate Street that he entertained Queen Elizabeth when she visited the Exchange, and ordered it to be called "Royal." She had already had experience of Gresham's courtier-like devotion as a host, for only in the preceding year she had been his guest at his country house at Osterley, when an incident occurred that showed his determination to please her.

The Queen had remarked that the court of his house was too large, and that it would look better if divided into two. Instantly Sir Thomas despatched messengers to procure workmen, and in the night-time a wall was run up in the middle; so that in the morning the Queen, to her surprise, found the work which she had suggested actually achieved.

It was in the beginning of the year 1565— counting the new style—that Gresham made the proposal to the Court of Aldermen that if they would provide him with a suitable plot of ground he would build the Bourse or Exchange which was so much wanted. Often, by-the-by, in reading of those times we come upon a sort of double date which puzzles people who do not know what it means. Thus the event we are considering is often mentioned as happening in the year 1564–5. Until the alteration of style which took place in the eighteenth century, and which was necessary to make the measurement of the year astronomically correct, it seemed the habit to consider that the old year ran on until the vernal equinox, which takes place in March. This is why the second figure is necessary to indicate to modern readers what was meant, or we might easily make the mistake of a year in regard to events occurring in January, February, or March.

Now the inconvenience of transacting business in all weathers in the open air had long been felt; besides, it was a time of great tribulation to foreign traders in consequence of the wars in France and the Low Countries, and this circumstance had perhaps something to do with hastening on affairs. Driven from their own country, often by religious persecution, these men came to England, where they knew protestants would be safe, bringing money with them and very often skill in various arts. Not only did they seem surprised that the English merchants had no proper accommodation, but their coming increasing the number of merchants made the want of a suitable building all the more inconvenient. So you see it was a very good time for Sir Thomas Gresham to make his proposal.

The Court of Aldermen readily entered into the scheme and set about raising the necessary money by a subscription, to which no less than seven hundred and fifty citizens contributed. Certain houses in Cornhill and Broad Street, with three alleys, were purchased by the citizens of London, the houses pulled down and the materials carted away; and when the plot of ground was made clear it was formally given in the name of the whole body of citizens to " Sir Thomas Gresham Knight agent to the Queen's Highness thereupon to build a bourse or place for merchants to assemble in at his own proper charges. And he on the 7th June (1566) laying the first stone of the foundation being brick accompanied with some aldermen, every one of them laid a piece of gold, which the workmen took up, and forthwith followed upon the same with such diligence, that by the month of November in the year 1567 the same was covered with slate, and shortly after fully finished."

These are the words of the quaint old chronicler Stow; and there is no doubt that Gresham undertook all the risk and responsibility of the building. It is believed, however, that he was somewhat assisted by his friend Clough, who was also a rich man; but if so it was by a bequest rather than a donation, and apparently without any desire on the testator's part to have such assistance publicly acknowledged. The two men had been intimately associated in a variety of undertakings for many years.

Gresham, who was always shrewd and practical, set about the work he had undertaken in the most business-like manner. The freestone used in the building was brought from one of his estates, and the timber from another ; and quite within the memory of man the remains of large saw-pits employed in sawing the timber for the Exchange were to be distinguished at Battisford Tye. Certain stones of a peculiar sort, the slates, iron work, glass, and wainscot seem in a great measure to have been brought from Antwerp ; and Gresham's architect was a Fleming named Henrich. Many of the common labourers also came from the Low Countries, Gresham having stipulated that he should be allowed to engage foreigners.

This aroused the jealousy of the English workmen, and some rioting ensued; but Gresham knew the Flemings well, and it is little likely that he would have chosen them for his workmen without good reason. It is a very old story that of the English being jealous of foreigners, and not believing that they had anything to learn from them; and perhaps the mass of the people were not aware that their new Exchange was a close imitation of Antwerp Bourse.

There are pictures still extant of the first exchange in which the resemblance can be traced; but one peculiarity has always belonged to the English edifice, and that is the association of the grasshopper with it. This was Gresham's crest, of which he seemed very proud. It was the sign of his house in Lombard Street; he used it constantly as a seal; and he not only decorated the four corners of the exchange with it, but the lofty square tower which could be seen from a distance was surmounted by a ball and grasshopper.

There has been a great deal of curiosity, and

even controversy, about this crest.   There was a silly tradition, which for some time prevailed, that Gresham had been a deserted child on the point of perishing from neglect, when attention was aroused to him by the chirping of a grass-hopper, and that he had adopted the crest out of gratitude to the little creature.   But this story is utterly without foundation, because it is clearly proved not only that the Greshams were people of some consequence for generations before Sir Thomas was born, but that they had habitually used the crest in question.   In all probability it was adopted as a sort of pun on the name Gresham, which would not need much alteration to mean in the old Anglo-Saxon " grass home."   A home in the grass is certainly that of the grasshopper ; and perhaps even the surname of Gresham itself may have originated from some grassy locality.   When you study heraldry —which to those who love history and biogra-phy is a most interesting subject—you will find many instances of what the French call *armes parlantes*, the English canting heraldry, in which the crest or some part of the arms has refer-

ence to the name of the person entitled to use
it. Pride in their crest seems to have been
quite ingrained in the Gresham family, for
Isabella, Lady Gresham, the second wife of Sir
Richard, and consequently stepmother to Sir
Thomas, among other legacies was able to be-
queath to him "a counterpoint (counterpane)
of fine imagery with grasshoppers" and likewise two carpets with the family crest woven in
them.

The original Exchange was so constructed
as to have a number of shops besides the ample
covered walks and rooms for the merchants, and
no doubt Gresham calculated on the rents paid
for these shops proving good interest for his
outlay. But for some time he was disappointed;
the shops let but slowly, and it is thought that
the famous visit of Queen Elizabeth was planned in order that her presence might have a
good effect. Gresham himself visited those few
shopkeepers who had taken shops, entreating
them to set out their wares to the best advantage, and put wax lights in the windows of as
many shops as they could, in readiness for the

Queen's visit, promising that in return they should be rent free for a year.

The Exchange was absolutely finished and used by merchants in 1569, though the Queen's visit was not until 1571. It was on a January day in this year that Queen Elizabeth came in great state and attended by her chief nobility to Gresham's House in Bishopsgate Street, where she dined. The dinner hour of course was early, according to the custom of the time, and it was after dinner that the Queen with great pomp examined the new Exchange, and visited the shops where the wares were set off to advantage by wax light. It is to be hoped she made some purchases, or if she did not that the courtiers who followed in her train patronized the new traders, otherwise after all their trouble they must have been rather disheartened. However this might be, her Majesty desired by proclamation with herald and trumpet, that the building should be called the Royal Exchange and "not otherwise."

Reading of that eventful day one feels curious about many things. Gresham was in high

THE ROYAL EXCHANGE.

favour with the Queen, but she had given him one proof of her trust in him that could not have been very agreeable. She had entrusted to him the custody of a poor lady who had the misfortune—for such to her it was—to belong to the Tudor family. This was the Lady Mary Grey, sister of Lady Jane Grey who died on the scaffold, great grand-daughter of Henry the Seventh and consequently cousin to Queen Elizabeth. She had offended the Queen by her marriage, and had been forcibly separated from her husband; her sister, Lady Catherine, having been subjected to similar treatment for a similar offence. The cruel treatment of these ladies was without any just excuse; though it was accounted for by the dread of them or their children as future pretenders to the crown. In all history it would be hard to find three more unfortunate sisters than these three ladies.

At the time Elizabeth visited the Exchange, and dined at Gresham's house in Bishopsgate Street, the Lady Mary Grey was a prisoner there. One would like to know if any grace were awarded her on the occasion, or any opportunity given the captive to plead her cause. Probably not. Probably she remained in some apartment far away from the banquet hall, out of sight and out of mind of the revellers, though perhaps not too remote to hear the stir and bustle of the memorable occasion.

The Royal Exchange was decorated with many statues of kings and queens; and a statue of Gresham was also erected there. It is a curious circumstance that when the Royal Exchange was burnt to the ground in the great fire of London in 1666 the statue of Gresham, " though fallen from its niche, remained entire, when all those of the kings since the Conquest were broken to pieces."

Much as the citizens must have had on their hands to restore after the great fire, they promptly set about rebuilding their Exchange. The first stone of the new edifice was laid on the 6th May 1667, and on the 23rd of October in the same year Charles the Second went with his "kettle-drums and trumpets" in royal state to lay the base of one of the columns, and afterwards was regaled sumptuously by the city magnates. It is pleasant to add that he gave £20 in gold to be distributed among the workpeople, a sum equivalent to four or five times as much now. In the uncovered quadrangle of the new building a statue of Charles the Second was placed; but the statue of Sir Thomas Gresham, the original founder, instead of being given a place of honour, was put under the north piazza, and so neglected that it was commonly, covered with placards and advertisements.

The Exchange erected in the reign of Charles the Second was destined like its predecesor to be consumed by fire. On the night of Wednesday, January the 10th, 1838, it fell a victim to the flames, involving, in the destruction of shops and warehouses attached to it, incalculable loss. A circumstance is related in connection with this fire which must have had a strange effect at the time. The clock of the Exchange at certain hours chimed certain tunes. The tune for Wednesday was the well-known one attached to the Scotch song " There is nae luck about the house," and while the fire was raging the bells rang out the sadly appropriate air and then fell one after another into the ruin beneath.

We must now briefly describe the present Royal Exchange, which as yet is too new to have many historical associations. Yet like its predecessors the building was inaugurated by royalty, the first stone having been laid by the late lamented Prince Consort, on January 17th, 1842, and the edifice opened by her Majesty Queen Victoria, October the 28th, 1844. Both events were of course occasions of much state and ceremony. This noble edifice was built from designs by the architect William Tite, and consists .of an open court or quadrangle surrounded by a colonnade. A marble statue of Her Majesty by the late J. G. Lough, a work expressive of regal dignity, seems fitly to preside over the scene, while statues of Gresham, Queen Elizabeth and Sir Hugh Middleton are appropriately placed. It is worthy of note that certain small stones called the "Turkey stones" are used as pavement, being the original stones employed by Gresham, and probably brought by him from Antwerp.

On the architrave of the north façade of

the Exchange are inscriptions divided by a moulding. "The earth is the Lord's and the fulness thereof" was suggested by the Prince Consort. The inscription on the left of the spectator is the well-known city motto, "Domine dirige nos," and that on the right is "Honor Deo." The central compartment is occupied by the motto of Sir Thomas Gresham :—

"FORTUN A MY."

Behind the Royal Exchange is a statue in bronze of George Peabody, the American Philanthropist, by his countryman Story.

Lloyd's Subscription Rooms occupy a very important part of the Royal Exchange, and are intimately associated with the mercantile business of London. The entrance to them is in the area, near the Eastern Gate. A wide flight of stairs leads to a spacious vestibule, where are placed a marble statue of the Prince Consort by Lough, and one of Huskisson by Gibson, R.A. On the wall is a tablet erected as a testimonial to the proprietors of the *Times* for the energy and public spirit displayed in the exposure of a fraudulent conspiracy. In this vestibule are the entrances to the three principal subscription rooms, the Underwriters', the Merchants' and the Captains' rooms.

Though the building has been twice destroyed by fire the spot is the same as that which by Gresham's munificence was dedicated to commerce three centuries ago. Other merchant princes have trod the well-worn Turkey stones, many generations of men have arisen and passed away, but the "merchant adventurer" of the sixteenth century, the skilful financier, and worthy favourite of at least three Tudor sovereigns still lives in our memory as a munificent benefactor worthy of fame and lasting honour. The grasshopper still designates the original founder, with, to fancy's eye, a proud supremacy. Little likely indeed is it that while London lasts Gresham should ever be forgotten.

Sir Thomas Gresham died suddenly, apparently of apoplexy, on the 21st November, 1579, in the sixty-first year of his age. Coming from the Exchange to his house in Bishopsgate Street he fell down, was taken up speechless and shortly afterwards died. He was buried in St. Helen's Church, Bishopsgate Street, where his son Richard had been interred. His widow, who is represented as having been very avaricious, neglected to put even an inscription on his tomb, though he left her exceedingly rich. It was not until 1736 that, by order of the churchwardens, there was cut on the black marble slab which covered the alabaster tomb the following memorial :—

"Sir THOMAS GRESHAM, Knight,
Bury'd December 15th, 1579."

The tomb may still be seen. It is said, however, that the obsequies were very solemn and splendid, and were attended by a hundred poor men and a hundred poor women for whom rather costly mourning was provided.

Gresham left large sums of money by his will for various benevolent purposes; and he founded a college that was called by his name. Perhaps his widow thought that with so many memorials of his life he did not need any epitaph; perhaps she could not make up her mind what inscription to choose, and so died without coming to a decision. To be sure, as she lived seventeen years after her husband, it was a long time to take in making up her mind, but as she is not here to explain the reason for her neglect we may as well give her the benefit of the doubt.

THE TOWER.

N old writer, famous for his learning and his wit, says in allusion to the Pyramids of Egypt that " they are so old they have forgotten their founder ;" and a similar remark may justly be applied to the Tower of London. Authentic history goes back eight hundred years to the days of William the Conqueror, in whose reign without doubt great additions were made to the Tower ; but tradition assigns to it a more hoary antiquity, and many old chronicles give to Julius Cæsar the credit of the first erection. What food for the imagination there is in the conquest of England by the Romans ! In reading of it

we want to know so much more than historian
has ever told, and we go on questioning the
dumb evidences which remain till they seem
almost to find a tongue!

The probability is that the Romans did dig
the deep foundations of the building, and did
erect a strong fortress, that might prove if need
be a citadel of defence, and a vantage ground to
protect the water way of the Thames. To this
may have been added the most important parts
of the Tower, mainly from the designs of the
Norman monk Gundulf, in the eleventh century;
and under the direction of King Henry the
Third in the thirteenth century. On both
occasions the work was very costly and the
people grumbled at the taxes which were levied
to meet the expense. But William the Conqueror was not much concerned at impotent
discontent, and Henry the Third had so much
the passion of an architect that he was surnamed "the Builder."

One of the traditions connected with the
Tower was that the mortar with which it was
cemented was moistened by the blood of beasts.

An idle story no doubt, but one more likely to
have been invented in connection with the
Romans, than to have arisen in Christian times.
It is worthy of remark that this tradition was
extant long before the Tower became the scene
of murder and judicial death.

To describe all that is known of the erection of the Tower of London—its walls of many
feet thickness, its numerous compartments, its
State chambers, and its dismal dungeons, would
alone make a volume ; and one which, after all,
would give but a feeble idea of the place unless
it were closely interwoven with the history of
England for many centuries. In mediæval times
it was a common thing for the dungeons of
State prisoners to be under the roof of a palace,
and for hundreds of years the Tower of London
was used alike as a royal residence and a State
prison. Often, too, it was considered a citadel
to be defended ; as when during Richard Cœur
de Lion's absence in the Holy Land, Long-
champ held the Tower against the rebellious
John and his partisans. Again, Henry the Third
and his Queen took refuge in the Tower from

De Montford and the associated Barons.   And
here it may be mentioned that it was Henry
the Third who first introduced wild beasts into
this stronghold.   Three leopards had been presented to him by the Emperor Frederick, and for
safe keeping they were brought to the Tower.

In those days but few people travelled, and
pictorial art was in so low a state that accurate
delineations of such creatures must have been
very rare.   We can fancy, therefore, what an
interesting sight these animals must have been,
and can understand how, for centuries, the custom was kept up of caging lions and tigers in
a compartment called the Lion Tower.   Quite
within the memory of elderly people, wild beasts
were kept in the Tower, and were considered
one of the sights of London for country people
to visit.   But that was before the Zoological
Gardens were established ; and all humane people
and lovers of animals must, I think, rejoice that
wild creatures are now more kindly treated than
it was possible for them to be under the former
conditions.   Poor things ! confinement must be
hard for them under any circumstances, and they

pay dearly for the opportunity they give us of studying their habits.

It is very likely that the cant phrase of "seeing the lions" originated at the time when visiting the lions in the Tower was thought quite an event by country people; the creatures being found so surprising, that in the course of time any strange and wonderful thing got the nickname of "a lion."

The Tower was used not only as a palace and a prison, but as a place of justice—if so it deserved to be called in days when law was often very undefined, and when the wise and right were apt to be warped aside by bribery and corruption of many sorts. Here, too, deliberate murder was more than once committed. The room is still shown in which the sons of Edward the Fourth were said to have been smothered by the orders of their usurping uncle Richard the Third. It is true that some historians have thrown doubt on the story of the "murder of the Princes in the Tower," but the prevailing opinion is that the bones discovered in the Tower in 1674 were those of the unfortunate children. In the

Tower, also, Sir Thomas Overbury was certainly murdered in the reign of James I.

Here Anne Boleyn was received with the pomp and deference becoming to a Queen; and here, three years later, she came as a prisoner, only to be released by death. Here the hapless Lady Jane Grey received homage as "the nine days' Queen;" and here she lingered for months as a prisoner before she also mounted the scaffold and closed her noble life, leaving for all time a blameless and heroic memory. Here Cranmer, Ridley and Latimer were imprisoned before their martyrdom. Here the poet-prince, Charles of Orleans, spent twenty-five years of his life, till that time after his capture the enormous ransom fixed on his head was paid. Here Edward Courtney spent the flower of his youth, for no sin, but for the misfortune of being too near the throne. Here the great Elizabeth became a prisoner to her sister Mary, and it is related that as she stepped on shore she turned and said, with much solemnity, "Here landeth as true a subject, being a prisoner, as ever landed at these stairs; and before

Thee, O God, I speak it." A few, very few years, and Mary was no more; and the some time prisoner was the great Queen, stong enough to guide safely the State, like the helmsman a ship, through perils many and varied.

But perhaps if we remember all the bearings of his history the Tower never contained a more remarkable inmate than Sir Walter Raleigh. His great and varied talents and acquirements, his romantic and adventurous life, his high prosperity and deep adversity, his courage and energy in the days of action, and his courage and patience in pain and degradation render his life a study alike profitable and interesting.

Raleigh was born in the year 1552 at Hayes in the parish of Budley in Devonshire. His father, though not rich, was a gentleman of good family, and Walter was started in life with that best endowment, a good education. After due preparatory training, he was entered a commoner at Oriel College, Oxford, where he greatly distinguished himself, being considered, as it is quaintly recorded, "a worthy proficient in oratory and philosophy." As early, however, as

his eighteenth year he joined a band of gentlemen volunteers whom Queen Elizabeth autho-
rized to serve in France, and assist the Hugue-
nots then contending for liberty of worship. He
was absent for years, taking part in several
memorable engagements, studying the science of
war as it was then understood, and storing his
mind with the observation of men and manners.
Though still very young when he returned to
England, he was soon recognized as a man likely
to be a leader.

There is a story told, which may or may not
be true, of his happening to be near Queen Elizabeth when her progress in walking was impeded
by the miry state of the pathway, and of the
young courtier promptly stripping off his rich
cloak and flinging it down for the Queen to step
on. There seems nothing unlikely in the incident thus recorded. Our Plantagenet and Tudor
sovereigns—when popular—were accustomed to
be served on bended knee, and with an almost
slavish adulation ; but apart from the loyalty of
a subject to his Queen, the action was that of a
gallant gentleman to a lady, and was no doubt

one that Elizabeth would have appreciated.
However this may be, he soon became a favourite,
for Queen Elizabeth had in a remarkable degree
the faculty of discerning merit.

That he was ambitious, there is no doubt, and
a just ambition is never to be blamed. It is
recorded that in the early days of his court
favour he scratched with a diamond on the pane
of a window which the Queen was likely to see,

"Fain would I climb, yet fear I to fall,"

and that Her Majesty completed the couplet by
adding,

"If thy heart fails thee climb not at all."

" However," says Fuller, " he at last climbed up
by the stairs of his own desert." And indeed
his merits were truly great, though he was not
without faults.

There are many indications that Raleigh was
a very far-seeing politician. Through life he
was the unflinching enemy of Spain, perceiving
always that it was a power which by avowed
antagonism, no less than by cunning measures,
was opposed to the freedom of thought and

action, which Englishmen had fought and suffered to secure, and which was but the stepping
stone to the wiser laws and fuller liberty which
we now enjoy. This passionate hatred of the
Spaniard, or rather of the policy which the
Spanish Government represented, accounts for
some blamable actions in Raleigh's life though
it does not excuse them; yet in judging of his
severity towards enemies we must remember
how much less was thought of the sacredness of
human life in the sixteenth century than happily
is the case at present.

Raleigh's detestation of Spain and Spanish
influence was closely allied to another mastering
passion of his life. This was his desire to
explore and colonize in America, then and long
afterwards called the New World. After serving in France and the Netherlands to uphold
the Protestant cause he made an unsuccessful
attempt to establish a colony in North America,
and on his return home in 1579, he entered the
Queen's army and proceeded to Ireland to quell
the rebellion there, the Spaniards helping the
rebels.

But the desire for adventure across the Ocean still possessed him. After careful study of such rude maps of the newly discovered continent as then existed, and after consultation with seamen and authorities on whom he could rely, he was persuaded that there remained much undiscovered land north of the Gulf of Florida. He procured the assent of the Queen in Council to the expedition he was planning, and she gave him letters patent granting to him and his heirs property in such lands as he might discover. This time he was successful—he returned home in triumph, was knighted by the Queen, and rewarded by a patent for licensing the sale of wine throughout the country; while Elizabeth directed that the state which had been added to her possessions should be called Virginia—the name it bears to this day. As Raleigh had fitted out two ships for the expedition at his own cost he must have well deserved such reimbursement.

Afterwards he organized other expeditions, and had compensation for the outlay perhaps in the fine estate in Ireland which was granted him

I

out of the forfeited lands.   Moreover, he is said
to have had rich prizes captured from the Spaniards, and we hear of him as sumptuously attired,
his tall and handsome person sparkling with
jewels of great value.

For many succeeding years Raleigh was a
prominent figure at the English court.   He
entered Parliament, and distinguished himself in a variety of ways.   Colonization in
America proceeded under his auspices, and
through some of the expeditions of the time
tobacco and the potato were introduced into
Europe.   The first cultivation of the potato on
this side of the Atlantic is said to have been on
Sir Walter's estates in Ireland.   There is an
amusing story told of a servant of his being
dreadfully frightened on first seeing Raleigh
smoke tobacco, the man believing his master to
be on fire.

The defeat of the Spanish Armada is too
great a subject to be more than glanced at here.
Every reader of English history remembers
the event, but it requires no little knowledge of
the complications of the time to fully understand

its importance. The attempted invasion was a desperate scheme to overthrow liberty in England and re-establish Popery, and rarely has any country had such an opportunity of showing the true character and patriotism of its people as England had then. From the Queen to the humblest of her subjects the enthusiasm of the nation was unbounded; all with one accord were determined to resist the haughty, bigoted, and cruel Spaniards to the death. When the Queen asked from the City of London the aid of five thousand men and fifteen ships, it voted thirty ships and ten thousand men; and nobles and men of fortune fitted out ships at their own expense to oppose the enemy. Raleigh was of the number who did this in a liberal and patriotic spirit, few men of that day perhaps so well understanding the importance of the crisis.

Macaulay in one of his stirring ballads tells how the beacons were lighted all over England to warn people of the approach of the Armada. You must remember there were no railroads, no electric telegraphs in those days, and in the usual course news travelled only as fast as a horseman could carry it. Therefore it was arranged that when the enemy was known to be approaching, signal fires should be lighted on hill tops near the coast; these were seen at the distance of many miles, and when recognized were responded to by similar beacon flames which in their turn were seen more inland and repeated; so that in a short time the whole country was apprised of its danger and up in arms.

"From Eddystone to Berwick bounds, from Lynn to Milford
      Bay,
That time of slumber was as bright and busy as the day;
For swift to east and swift to west the ghastly war-flame spread:
High on St. Michael's Mount it shone; it shone on Beachy
      Head.
Far on the deep the Spaniards saw, along each southern
      shire—
Cape beyond cape, in endless range, those twinkling points of
      fire.
          *   *   *   *   *
The sentinel on Whitehall gate looked forth into the night
And saw o'erhanging Richmond Hill the streaks of blood-red
      light.
Then bugle's note and cannon's roar the death-like silence
      broke,
And with one start, and with one cry the royal city woke.
At once on all her stately gates arose the answering fires;
At once the wild alarum clashed from all her reeling spires."

So says Macaulay; and even his glowing poetry does not exaggerate the enthusiasm of the people, or the spirited manner in which they showed their patriotism.

It does not need a very great stretch of imagination to picture Raleigh's delight at the defeat of the Armada. Perhaps for the first time he felt assured that England would come out finally victorious over cruel tyranny and oppression, however hard the struggle yet might prove to be.

The next few years of Raleigh's life were full of change. He offended the Queen and was for a time banished the court, but after his marriage to one of her Maids of Honour he was comparatively restored to favour. He resided for some time on his Irish property, and during this time renewed his intimacy with Spenser, the author of "The Fairy Queen." In 1595 he again sailed for the New World in search of the fabled El Dorado, where it had been rumoured there were mines of inexhaustible wealth. He left his ships at the mouth of the Orinoco, and sailed up the river four hundred miles in boats. It is pleasant to know that he treated the Indians with humanity and kindness, which strongly contrasted with the savage cruelty which they had experienced from the Spaniards. Indeed, his name was remembered with gratitude by them long after he had departed.

The rainy season approaching, however, he was obliged to return without having discovered the land of wealth; but he had acquired geographical knowledge which was most valuable to future explorers, and he returned to England more convinced than ever of the importance of establishing colonies in America. In 1596 Raleigh had a high command in the expedition which resulted in the destruction of the Spanish Fleet in the harbour of Cadiz, a naval achievement which was considered due to his skill and judgment. Soon afterwards he became a Rear-Admiral, and for the remainder of Queen Elizabeth's reign the tide of his prosperity set steadily in. But Secretary Cecil hated him with the persistent hatred of envy; and finding Elizabeth, even in her old age, too shrewd to alter her estimate of Raleigh's worth, he set himself to undermine the hero with her successor.

When the great Queen died, and the Scottish

James ascended the throne, that policy which must always remain the glory of England was at once reversed. There was to be no more help to the Low Countries against the tyranny of Spain, and no more resistance of the aggression of that power in the Old World or New—supposing always that it did not threaten England with a fresh Armada. Negotiations—which happily came to nothing—were set on foot for the marriage of an English prince with a Spanish Infanta, James being greatly tempted thereto by the promise of an enormous dowry with the bride.

It is to the honour of the Queen, Anne of Denmark, wife of James the First, that she was not tempted by the glittering bait, was never in favour of the match. Moreover, she was the persistent friend of Raleigh, however powerless to serve him.

It is impossible to understand the cabals which led to Raleigh's long imprisonment in the Tower without realizing the conflict which raged between the two political parties in the early days of the new King's reign. Narrow minded and pusillanimous, James had no sympathy with the oppressed, and no chivalry of feeling to hinder his alliance with the oppressor. But there were a few finer spirits, of whom perhaps Raleigh was the chief, that chafed at the degradation of breaking promises to allies and fawning upon the powerful Spaniard. Though little is said on the subject, it is likely enough that he was indiscreet in his speech, and so became a sort of scapegoat, but there really is no evidence that he had anything to do with what in history is called the Arabella Plot. Lord Cobham, who was his accuser, recanted over and over again, though it was to his supposed complicity that Raleigh owed his condemnation and long imprisonment in the Tower.

It must be remembered that James the First was distinctly the legitimate heir to the throne of England. By both his parents, Mary Queen of Scots and her husband Darnley, James was descended from Margaret Tudor, the daughter of Henry the Seventh ; but Darnley had a younger brother who was the father of Arabella Stuart. The only plea in her favour—and it was a very

flimsy one—was that James was an alien by
birth.

It was a great misfortune for this poor young
lady that she was so nearly allied to royalty, for
she was clever and amiable, and popular with all
who knew her, and for her own part only desired the natural freedom of a subject. None
knew better than herself that she had no right
to the throne of her cousin the King, but she
could not help crack-brained people talking treason in connection with her name. Among these
was Lord Cobham, who, when himself accused
of treason, implicated Raleigh in the supposed
"plot." Raleigh, as well as Lord Cobham, was
imprisoned in the Tower; but, of course, the
two were not allowed to meet. When Cecil—
Raleigh's bitter enemy—came to the Tower to
receive the final depositions of Cobham, the
latter retracted every word of his accusation—
positively declaring that Raleigh had never
asserted Arabella's claims, or spoken of Spanish
help in the matter.

Remembering Raleigh's avowed enmity to
Spain, it is really preposterous to suppose that

he should have planned any scheme in conjunction with that power.

About this time, while he was in confinement in the Tower, a report was spread that Raleigh attempted suicide, but there is not any proof that such was the fact. Raleigh at this time was full of strength and vigour, and hope of many earthly things—not at all a man likely to be led into such a sin; though had he purposed it, he was of too resolute a character to have failed. The probability is that the rumour of his death—for at first it was that—was spread by his enemies to ascertain how the nation would receive such news, and thus, in some measure, to learn how far it would be safe to make him a victim.

But the circumstances which led to Raleigh's long imprisonment in the Tower, if fairly narrated, would themselves make a book. Lord Cobham seems to have been one of those contemptible persons who, boastful and arrogant in prosperity, are cravens in adversity. He asserted things one day and denied them the next, in the hope of saving himself; so that no sensible person could place any reliance on what he said. It was this vacillation which compromised Raleigh, and gave Cecil and others the opportunity to injure him. There is also reason to believe that some supposed copies of letters of his are forgeries.

Sir Walter Raleigh, and the other so-called conspirators, were taken to Winchester in November, 1603, to be tried for high treason, and were found guilty and condemned to death. James even signed the death-warrants of three; and Markham, Grey and Cobham were brought to the scaffold, but respited after each respectively had gone through the bitterness of the last preparations for death. Raleigh was to have died three days later, but his sentence was commuted to imprisonment in the Tower during the King's pleasure. A like sentence was pronounced on the Lords Grey and Cobham, but the latter appears, after some time, to have escaped, and to have died in extreme poverty, wanting the very necessaries of life. Lord Grey was more carefully kept, and survived as a prisoner till 1614. Sir Griffin Markham was banished from England.

The estates of the conspirators were confiscated to the King, though a certain allowance was made for their support in the Tower; and now began that long term of imprisonment which must for ever associate the name of Raleigh—the scholar and poet, the seaman and soldier and statesman—with the old Fortress. It is true he was allowed the solace of his wife's companionship, and he was permitted to see certain of his friends, but the history of those twelve years is pathetic in the extreme. One by one his calamities accumulated. As you may remember, Queen Elizabeth, in reward for his services, granted him a wine patent—a power of granting licenses—which was a considerable source of income to him; this was taken away. Then his mansion of Durham House was confiscated; and next, James wanting an estate to bestow on his new favourite, Robert Carr, seized on Sherborne Castle, though Raleigh had settled the succession of this beautiful place on his elder son. The King found, or pretended to

find, some flaw in the settlement, and insisted on having the estate; and when Lady Raleigh threw herself at the Monarch's feet imploring him not to take "the bread from her children's mouths," he was insensible to her distress, and roughly answered in his broad Scotch dialect—

"Madam, I maun ha' it; I maun ha' it for Carr."

Poor Lady Raleigh seems to have chafed under the great trouble more than her husband did. With greater truth than most men he might exclaim, " My mind to me a kingdom is; " and with his books and chemical apparatus he for a long time endured his imprisonment bravely —so bravely that his wife scarcely understood his fortitude and almost reproached him with it.

It was during his long confinement that his scientific researches were most remarkable. Happily he was not wholly debarred from prosecuting studies that every one saw might lead to results beneficial to mankind. Certain it is that he concocted a potion called "The Great Cordial," which for several generations was held in high esteem. The reigning Queen believed

that it had saved her life, and both Charles the
First and Charles the Second had great faith in
it. But his most precious discovery was the
means of extracting the brine from sea water,
and thus obviating the too common misery of a
sea voyage in days when navigation was far
more uncertain, and sea voyages were much
longer than they are at present. Unhappily the
secret of the process died with him only to be
recovered in recent times.

The fame of the prisoner spread far and wide.
Great ladies come to visit him and beg for his
cordial, and the heir apparent to the throne,
Prince Henry, delighted in his society. It was
said to have been expressly for him that Raleigh
began his History of the World, a splendid
fragment which remains to this day a monument of his learning and genius. In fact there
appears to have existed a genuine attachment
between the two, far more like that of master
and beloved pupil than that of a commoner and
royalty. The Prince was full of enthusiasm for
heroic deeds, and loved to hear Raleigh's account
of his adventures, and once, when leaving the

Tower, he was heard to exclaim, "No man but my father would keep such a bird in a cage."

But this promising young Prince died suddenly, and the shock and sorrow to Raleigh were great indeed. The next son of James, he who afterwards came to the throne as Charles the First, stepped into his brother's place at the English Court, but we do not hear of any special sympathy shown by him towards the illustrious prisoner.

Years passed by and there was no sign of Raleigh's release being at hand. His health had often suffered seriously from his confinement, from anxiety of mind and from hardships which, though a prisoner, he ought to have been spared.

At one time he was even turned out of his still-room, denied his usual "walk," and locked up in his room long before night. Lady Raleigh and their two sons, Walter and Carew, were sent away from the Tower, and in a hundred ways the imprisonment was now made more painful than ever.

Dwelling in a stone room, with insufficient

fire, no wonder the active man, accustomed to out-of-door exercise, sea breezes, and warm climates, broke down in health. Indeed his sufferings were so acute that even his enemies had some compassion on him, sending a physician to see him. The doctor declared his lodging to be too cold for any man to sleep in, and described the state of the patient as one of great distress. Raleigh seemed every second or third night to lose the use of his limbs, perhaps for two or three hours, and even his tongue became so numbed that he could not speak. Though under judicious treatment he in a great measure recovered, he acquired an ague to which he was always subject.

The physician's report occasioned the necessary change, and henceforth Raleigh was allowed to live in the Garden House among his books, retorts, and scientific instruments. Probably it was at this time that he wrote many of the poems which have been preserved, and the following verse of a little piece which is called a hymn may fairly be considered to represent his prevailing state of mind.

"Rise, oh, my Soul, with thy desires to Heaven,
And with Divinest contemplation use
Thy time, where Time's eternity is given,
And let vain thoughts no more thy thoughts abuse;
But down in darkness let them lie :
To live thy better, let thy worse thoughts die !"

Even as a prisoner Sir Walter Raleigh was to a certain extent a power in the State. From the Tower he sent forth writings on Ships and the Sea Service and various important subjects, such as probably no other man then living could have produced. It was well known that he still sighed after action, and had not lost his faith in the wonderful riches to be found in the New World. His pen, his voice, his personal influence had weight even in his prison, and in March, 1615, he obtained his release from the Tower with the avowed object of organizing an expedition to Guiana—not, however, without bribing the uncles of the then favourite George Villiers It was an age of terrible corruption, when court favour was almost openly bought and sold.

No sooner was Raleigh a free man than he urged the expediency of carrying out his plans,

K

offering out of the wreck of his fortune to bear
the chief burthen of the expense. Obtaining
the royal sanction, and a commission under the
privy seal, he set sail in command of a squadron
of thirteen ships. His aim was to colonize
Guiana in South America, and enrich England
with its mineral wealth. But Raleigh was now
upwards of sixty years of age ; it was evident
that his constitution had been shattered by the
hardships of his long imprisonment, and on reaching Guiana he became so ill that he could proceed no further. He, however, deputed Captain
Keymis to sail on up the river Orinoco in search
of treasure. This proceeding brought the expedition in conflict with the Spaniards, and though
Keymis was successful in an engagement and
took the town of St. Thomas, so far from the
victory being an advantage, it led to embroilment
of the two governments ; for it had been an
understood thing, that the English were not to
interfere with the Spanish settlements.

In the attack on St. Thomas, Raleigh's elder
son and namesake was killed. He was a youth of
great promise, and with not a little of his father's

ardour and impetuosity of character ; he was in fact reckless of his life, and thus lost it.

One would think that even Raleigh's bitterest enemies must have been touched by compassion for him under his accumulated sorrows. As for the unhappy Keymis, his mind gave way under the disappointment of his failure—and perhaps some stinging reproaches from Raleigh—and he committed suicide. Raleigh the great admiral returned to England worn out in body and sick of heart, to find, of course, that ill news had travelled before him, and that the failure of the expedition was looked upon as a capital crime. Just then a treaty was on foot for a marriage of Prince Charles with the Spanish Infanta— though, as we know, it never took place—and the English Government was intent before all things on conciliating Spain. Philip's Ambassador was instructed to urge the punishment of Raleigh, ostensibly for the attack on St. Thomas, but really because he had always been recognized as the unswerving enemy of Spain. Arrived at Plymouth, Raleigh was arrested, brought to

London, and once more committed a prisoner to the Tower.

Here he was very narrowly watched, in the hope of detecting something in his correspondence which could be brought forward as a new fault ; but the Government failing in this, it was determined that the sentence passed on him fifteen years before should now be carried out. The lawyers, however, urged that it was a very novel case, and that the prisoner should be allowed to plead for himself, why the sentence should not be executed. Accordingly, on the 28th October, 1618, he was brought from the Tower to the Court of King's Bench, where the record of his conviction was read. Raleigh knew well that he must die, for he was aware that the King of Spain was clamouring for his death—but he pleaded, nevertheless, that the former sentence must have been annulled when he received the king's commission to proceed to Guiana with full power of a Marshal. "By that commission," he observed, "I gained new life and vigour; for he that hath power over the lives of others, must surely be master of his own." Yet the Chief Justice overruled all his arguments and pathetic pleading, admitted that the prisoner was not called to execution in cold blood on the old sentence, but asserted that " new offences had stirred up his Majesty's justice to revive what the law had formerly granted."

Execution was ordered for the next day, October 29th, 1618, and though Raleigh pleaded hard for a brief respite, in order to settle some of his worldly affairs, the favour was denied him. Instead of returning to the Tower, he was taken to the Gate House at Westminster, where, in the evening, he took leave of his devoted wife. At eight o'clock next morning he was led to the scaffold in Palace Yard, where a great concourse of people were assembled. When Sir Walter appeared, he saluted the " lords, knights, and gentlemen," and spoke on the scaffold as a Christian and a patriot. The dying man forgave his enemies, but defended himself to the last from the charges which had brought him to the block. The morning being sharp, and some delay arising, the sheriff asked if he would like to warm himself at a fire, " No, good Mr. Sheriff," said he, "let us dispatch, for within this quarter of an hour mine ague will come upon me, and if I be not dead before then, mine enemies will say I quake for fear."

Then he poised the axe, and felt its edge, saying with a smile, "This is a sharp medicine, but it will cure all diseases." Seeing that, after he had laid his head on the block, the headsman hesitated, he exclaimed " What dost thou fear ? Strike, man."

Thus fell in the sixty-seventh year of his age Walter Raleigh the soldier and sailor, and statesman, the poet and historian, a man possessing noble qualities, and leaving a name that will for ever be illustrious.

The Lady Arabella Stuart, the innocent cause of so much suffering to others, and so hapless in her own life, was long a prisoner in the Tower —and for no deeper offence than marrying without the King's consent. Those were days in which the mere will of the Sovereign was in such matters law. She was forcibly separated from her husband, and after many fruitless attempts at escape and reunion, her mind gave way, and she died in the Tower—more from what is called a broken heart than from palpable disease. Hers is a long history and one full of painful interest.

There is no sign that Raleigh was of a revengeful nature; but perhaps before he died he felt the force of the retribution which had overtaken his old enemy Robert Carr. That sometime favourite of James the First, created first Lord Rochester and then Earl of Somerset, became, with his worthless wife, a prisoner in the Tower, charged with instigating the murder of Sir Thomas Overbury. He, the despoiler for whose sake Sherborne Castle had been confiscated, was in his turn disgraced and impoverished —but the bad pair deserved their fate and lived and died unpitied.

Sir Walter Raleigh's only surviving son— Carew—born in the Tower in 1604, lived till 1666, seeing many vicissitudes of fortune. He seems to have been an accomplished gentleman, who travelled on the continent in his youth. He revered his father's memory and vindicated it with his pen. He was buried in his father's grave in St. Margaret's, Westminster.

THE GREAT PLAGUE OF LONDON.

A.D. 1665.

THERE is a clause in the Litany of the Church of England in which we ask especially to be delivered from "plague, pestilence and famine; from battle and murder and from sudden death," and when we remember the ravages and terrible sufferings which from time to time Pestilence has occasioned, we feel how fitly it is placed among those great calamities from which we beseech God to spare us.

Every student of the Bible is aware how often the "noisome pestilence" was chronicled as a chastisement on the nations, or threatened as one; and profane history records with painful minuteness many visitations which have devastated and depopulated cities. "The Pestilence that walketh in darkness" has come to mankind at different epochs in different forms, but in its most malignant character it has for ages past been known as "The Plague."

Thucydides gives a vivid description of the plague which in the time of Pericles broke out in Athens. It was believed to have originated in Ethiopia; and then spread through Egypt and Persia till it reached the coast of Greece. The mortality in Athens was enormous, the city being overcrowded in consequence of the war that was raging. Men and women apparently in excellent health were suddenly stricken; some died quickly, others lingered for days in agony; and, if they finally recovered, it was often with memory gone, or a body mutilated by the loss of hand or foot. Paganism was no support to a people under such an affliction; finding that their gods were unable or unwilling to relieve their sufferings, the dying appear to have passed away without hope, while those who escaped plunged into excesses, which they called pleasure, to drown thought, and with the avowed object of snatching temporal enjoyment even though death might be hovering near.

Very differently the Romans seem to have felt in the early days of the Christian Church, when towards the close of the sixth century Rome was devastated by a pestilence. Gregory the First, deservedly called the Great, was then Pope, and he ordered a solemn penitential service to be held in St. Peter's to implore Almighty God to stay the plague. It was believed that in the preparatory procession the Pontiff saw, as in a vision, the figure of the Archangel Michael standing at the top of a fortress, and in the act of sheathing his sword as a symbol that the pestilence would be stayed. This tradition is still credited in the Roman Catholic Church, and to commemorate it a statue of the Archangel was erected, in the act described, just at the spot where the vision was presented. The fortress had been the Mausoleum of Hadrian, but for many centuries it has been called the Castle of St. Angelo, on account of this episode in its history. It is still one of the famous sights of Rome, and the figure of the Angel sheathing his sword, as seen in relief against the pure blue sky of Italy, is most impressive.

It was this same Gregory the Great of whom it is recorded that, before his elevation to the Papacy, on seeing some beautiful fair-haired slaves in the slave-market of Rome he inquired from what country they came, and on being told they were Angles—as the English were then called—he exclaimed, they would be angels if they were Christians. He did not forget the incident, and when he became Pope he sent Augustine to England to preach and plant Christianity.

This Pope Gregory also introduced the musical chant which still goes by his name, and he was in many respects one of the great lights of his age.

The next memorable visitation of pestilence in Italy was that of Florence, commemorated by Boccaccio, and which took place about the middle of the fourteenth century. More than a hundred years later, Milan was similarly afflicted, but on this occasion Carlo Borromeo, the noble-hearted Archbishop, so distinguished himself that he has left a deathless memory behind him. While still young he had proved himself a wise benefactor as the founder of hospitals and schools, and as the reformer of abuses ; but when the plague broke out in his diocese he visited the sick, and relieved their necessities in person, selling even the furniture of his house for the purpose, and setting a brave example to his clergy, and to all those who from selfish fear fled from danger, leaving the stricken sufferers to die in lonely misery. It is a time of trial like this which separates the generous and self-denying from the mean and cruel.

There was another terrible pestilence in 1633, said to have been occasioned by the miseries consequent on the wars of Gustavus Adolphus, and of which we have a periodical reminder when the Passion Play is acted at Ober-Ammergau. This little Bavarian village was almost depopulated, and the few surviving mourners besought

Almighty God to have mercy on them, and made
a vow that if the pestilence was stayed they
would have every ten years a theatrical representation "for thankful remembrance and edify-
ing contemplation, and by the help of the Creator" of "the sufferings of Jesus the Saviour of
the World." We are told that their prayer was
heard, "for not a single person died of the plague
after the vow was made, though many were
smitten by it."

Whatever we may think of the "edification"
to be derived from the spectacle of a Passion
Play, there is no doubt that these simple peasants regarded the performance much more in the
light of a religious service than a profanation :
and we must remember that miracle plays—or
plays on sacred subjects—were very common in
the middle ages.

It is, however, with the Great Plague of London, which broke out in 1665, that we have to
do. English history records many previous visitations of the pestilence, but nothing so terrible
as this. Pepys, in his Diary, mentions, as early
as 1663 and 1664, the rumours afloat of the

Plague raging in Holland, and precautions were taken by instituting a strict quarantine with regard to ships coming from infected seaports in November, 1663. But it is likely enough that the law was often evaded, and one unprincipled person who, for greed or pleasure landed in England without due precautions having been taken, might have spread the disease through a large community.

In those days people were less instructed than they are now with regard to those habits of life which promote health, or encourage sickness. There is good reason to believe that the mass of the people were not very cleanly, one reason having been that they wore heavier fabrics for garments than they do at present, and consequently their clothes, lasting much longer than thinner materials would have done, were less often changed. Thus the seeds of infection must frequently have lingered about the raiment of persons, and caused an outbreak of the malady when they were brought in contact with any one liable to receive it. Then, though London was more amply supplied with water than most cities, its inhabitants seem not to have used it very freely; but above all, the necessity of ventilation and proper drainage was but little understood. All these circumstances encouraged the Plague, a disease so dreadful that corruption of the body might almost be said to begin before life was extinct.

In September, 1664, Pepys records the news of a Dutch ship of three or four hundred tons burthen having been cast ashore at Gottenburgh, the entire crew being dead of the plague; and there is no doubt that it raged on the continent, and that there were even many isolated cases in England long before the outbreak which almost depopulated London. All through the spring, people watched the bills of mortality—that is the weekly account of the number of deaths—with painful interest, and spread the report of every case of plague that was mentioned. Week by week the deaths increased, and towards the end of May, when warm summer weather set in, there was an outburst of plague in St. Giles's, which quickly spread to adjacent parishes. The district of Whitehall, where Charles the

Second held his court, was threatened, and the city, in spite of many careful precautions, was very soon infected.

Now began the general flight of all those who were able to escape from the Metropolis and its neighbourhood. The nobility and gentry, who mostly had country houses of their own, were the first to flee, and the Royal Family soon followed their example. Indeed, all who had means at their disposal took refuge in the country. Certainly the most illustrious Englishman then living was of the number who thus fled; for John Milton with his family withdrew into Buckinghamshire, to a house engaged for him by a Quaker friend. Probably he was only just in time to escape danger, for in a few weeks the Lord Mayor refused to grant certificates of health, without which people were not permitted to leave the city; while at the same time the dwellers in country towns were resolute in turning back infected people. It was indeed a terrible time, when the dread which prompted self-defence generally triumphed over better feelings.

It is recorded that at this period the blind poet showed "Paradise Lost" to his Quaker friend Ellwood, and it is probable that the great poem was only then recently completed.

Of course the absence of all the wealthiest people from London caused a great stoppage of trade. Establishments were broken up, and it was said that not less than forty thousand servants were thrown out of employment. A still greater number of artisans and labourers were reduced to want. It is true that the rich gave large sums in charity. The King subscribed £1000 per week, and the City £600, to mitigate the distress; and the Archbishop of Canterbury, the Queen Dowager, and many of the nobility were extremely munificent—but still the distress which prevailed was very great. Unhappily the plague spread most rapidly among the poor who, weakened by their privations, were the least able to resist its attacks; but by them it was soon communicated to a higher rank, and before the end of June its ravages were so disastrous that the civil authorities thought it time to act upon the powers with which they were invested

They divided parishes into districts, and apportioned to each district a number of officers, namely searchers, examiners, watchmen, and nurses. They commanded that wherever the disease appeared the fact should be made known to the public by a red cross, one foot in length, being painted on the door with the words, *" Lord have mercy upon us,"* above it. From the moment this sign appeared the house was closed. For the space of one month no inmate was allowed to leave it, and thus whole families herded together were left to communicate the disease one to another. Many people, rendered desperate by this tyranny, either attempted to escape stealthily or to corrupt the watchmen whose duty it was to prevent their exit. No doubt some succeeded, and, with the Thames so near at hand, managed to escape, carrying the contagion with them.

Arrangements were made for the disposal of the dead. In the day officers were on the watch to remove the bodies of those who died in the street—for so sudden frequently was the seizure that death in the street was a quite common occurrence. At night the pest-cart went round, accompanied by links and the tinkling of a bell, and often with the mournful cry—" Bring out your dead!" Coffins were not used; mourners were not permitted to follow the remains of those they loved, nor was any funeral service read. The cart proceeded without delay to the nearest churchyard, where a large deep pit was dug, capable of holding many bodies. Here the cart was tilted, and the dead shot into the earth with as little ceremony as if they were but stones. When the churchyards were full, pits were dug in some other places. In times of general disaster the worst traits of human nature too often become apparent, and dreadful stories are told of the needless brutality of the men engaged in burying the dead. No doubt they were taken from a very low class, and in those days the lower classes were shockingly ignorant, and the new occupation of these men very soon hardened their hearts.

In July and August, as usual the two hottest months of the year, the weather was most oppres-sive, and the ravages of the pestilence became more and more terrible. Even men of strong mind and clear intellects became unnerved, while weaker characters seemed to lose all self-control. The most absurd rumours were circulated and believed. Among others, perhaps, the old idea was revived that malicious people brought the bad air of Turkey to England in bottles, which they opened in order to spread the disease. This was a notion which prevailed at an earlier period, when the plague had appeared in a milder form. The idea was extremely absurd, but Turkey was the home of the plague; and most probably it was first brought to England in the merchandise of the Levant traders.

Of course in the terrible summer of 1665 all communication with shipping was prohibited, and quite a little fleet of homeward-bound ships lay moored at the Nore and Medway, waiting for the pestilence to abate. Some coasting vessels bearing corn, butter, and eggs, were allowed to discharge their cargoes; and vessels from abroad sometimes managed to elude the vigilance of those in authority. Coals—which were greatly in demand, as the doctors ordered

THE PLAGUE.

large fires to be kept burning even in the hottest weather—rose to the enormous price of £4 per chaldron. Allowing for the difference in the value of money this would be something like £6 or £8 per ton.

It is a curious fact that, as was the case at the time of the pestilence in Rome, people fancied they saw a sword in the heavens. They declared it was of gigantic size—extending from Westminster to the Tower; and a comet which had appeared the preceding winter was remembered as a harbinger of evil. A strange star was also reported to have been seen, and these signs in the heavens were thought of with awe. Certain fanatics, believing themselves inspired, prophesied yet further calamities; and one of them, Solomon Eagle, almost unclothed, bearing on his head a pan of burning coals, walked through the streets declaring the judgments of God were on a sinful people, and that London in forty days would be destroyed.

It soon became impossible to carry out the orders of the magistrates. The nights were not long enough to bury all the dead in the first horrible manner, and burials in coffins now took place at all hours of the day. Also it was found that the very poor must perish from want if they were not permitted to leave their homes to seek relief. Those who had money often drew in their provisions at an upper window—but nothing from an infected house could be received without fumigation. Every letter was subjected to this process—sulphur being chiefly used, though hops, pepper, and frankincense, were also employed. Gunpowder likewise was exploded to purify the air.

London, indeed, presented a terrible picture of desolation. In the chief thoroughfares the grass grew freely; in some places whole rows of houses were tenantless; in others the red cross proclaimed the affliction within. From these, appalling cries of woe were often heard. The few persons who ventured to walk in the streets did so in the middle of the road, and when there was a prospect of their meeting each other they moved on one side to avoid contact.

In September, when the weather was a little cooler, people began to hope that the mortality would decrease; but they were disappointed. Indeed the disease became, if possible, more malignant. The Privy Council now ordered coal fires to be lighted in every street and alley of London and Westminster—one great fire to every twelve houses. These were kept burning three nights and days—at the end of which time they were extinguished by heavy rain.

The next week there was a happy diminution in the deaths, and the survivors rejoiced in the belief that the fires had swept away the pestilential miasma; but the following week the deaths again rose, carrying off no less than ten thousand victims—the largest number yet swept away in seven days. But the autumnal equinox was now at hand, and the high winds, customary at this period, blew with their wonted vigour, and purified the air—the disease became less malignant, the burials per week decreased from thousands to hundreds, and in December more than seventy districts were declared free from the plague. Thousands of people gladly returned to their homes, and in the following February, the King and his court were again established at

Whitehall. Isolated cases of plague, it is true, occurred for some years; but the population, thinned as it was by a hundred thousand deaths from the pestilence, soon resumed its old habits and congregated for business and pleasure. The grass in the thoroughfares was trodden down by a busy multitude, and we can understand what a mixture of sadness and rejoicing there must have been in the meeting of long-parted friends. Few households, indeed, could there have been in which there had not been some loss, and many must have been the thrilling tales survivors had to tell.

Pepys, in his "Diary," relates a touching incident of parents who, having lost all their children but one, and believing themselves doomed to die, "did desire only to save the life of this little child; and so prevailed to have it received stark naked into the arms of a friend, who brought it (having put it into new fresh clothes) to Greenwich; where, upon hearing the story, we did agree it should be permitted to be received and kept in the town."

But I am sure there must have been hundreds

of cases of parental devotion which were never recorded. Imagination cannot picture the dreadful scenes of suffering which must have been acted out in those closed houses on which the fatal seal was set. Sometimes even a large family was entirely swept away, and the pest-cart, night after night, received its burthen— sometimes a mourner or two remained still to be imprisoned in the house whence the beloved ones had been so hurriedly removed. For long years to come stories of the plague must have been current in every household.

Daniel Defoe, the author of "Robinson Crusoe," was but a child at the time, but he must have heard incidents recorded and descriptions of the visitation given—which sank deep into his mind. Only on this supposition can we realize, what is the truth, that his "Journal of the Plague in London" is but a work of imagination. But so vivid and truth-like is it, that for a long time it was received as a veritable history. Probably, though the personages introduced are fictitious, the incidents narrated are founded on fact, and all competent judges declare that, fiction though it be, it gives the most true and vivid picture of the Great Plague that exists.

More than two hundred years have passed since the dreadful visitation. Let us not presume on this long immunity, but still devoutly pray that from " plague, pestilence, and famine," our Merciful God will still deliver us !

THE GREAT FIRE OF LONDON.

A.D. 1666.

T has been aptly said that "fire is an excellent servant but a terrible master," and even a very slight burn will make us agree with the truth thus declared. But perhaps it is only a vast conflagration which sets us thinking of the power of an element which beyond all others is destructive; for even when most useful, and kept within due bounds, it still consumes that which feeds it—in other words—destroys.

In the early ages of the world fire, more than anything else, seems to have impressed the imagination of the heathen nations; witness the

sect of Fire-worshippers founded by Zoroaster,
and the mythological story of Prometheus.   In
his wrath with mankind Jupiter was supposed to
have deprived the earth of fire; but Prometheus
stole fire from the chariot of the sun, and
brought it back to the earth at the end of a
ferula, or hollow wand.   When we remember
the little knowledge that at that time was dif-
fused among the mass of mankind we can understand how pretty fables of this sort took hold of
the popular imagination.   The few wise men
then no doubt received them as we do now—as
types and symbols.

But in truth there has always been something
mysterious and stimulating to the mind in the
subject of fire.   Science teaches a great deal
about the laws of heat and combustion, but
when all is known that can be known, the
" devouring element" still remains unchanged in
its attributes.   To think even of a great conflagration is appalling when we attempt to follow out in fancy its absolute and most apparent
consequences.

In picturing the Great Fire of London we

must remember that in Charles the Second's reign, when it happened, the houses were chiefly of wood and thatched, and that most of the streets were very narrow. Indeed the sign-boards mentioned in the account of London Bridge, and which were so universal in the streets, often almost touched each other on opposite sides, and must have acted like great matches to set fresh houses on fire ; especially as many of them were pitched. We have to add, that the month of August had been especially hot and dry, so that every out-of-door combustible was parched and ready to catch the flames.

We owe much to those two famous diarists— Evelyn and Pepys—for their graphic accounts of many domestic events of the period ; but perhaps in no descriptions have they been more minute than when recording the outbreak and progress of the Great Fire. This is what Pepys says under the date Sept. 3rd :—

" *Lord's Day.*—Some of our maids sitting up late last night to get things ready against our feast to-day, Jane called us up about three in the morning to tell us of a great fire they saw in

the city. So I rose and went to her window;
and thought it to be on the back side of Mark
Lane at the farthest, but being unused to such
fires as followed I thought it far enough off;
and so went to bed again and to sleep. About
seven rose again to dress myself, and then looked
out at the window, and saw the fire not so much
as it was but further off. . . . By-and-by Jane
comes and tells me that she hears that above
three hundred houses have been burned down
to-night by the fire we saw and that it is now
burning down all Fish Street by London Bridge."

Then the writer describes going to the Tower,
and getting upon one of the high places, taking
Sir J. Robinson's little son with him, to have a
view of the dreadful sight. Thence he saw the
houses on London Bridge that were on fire.
From the Lieutenant of the Tower he heard
that the fire began at the King's baker's in Pud-
ding Lane, and that besides most part of Fish
Street it had already burnt down St. Magnus's
Church. In a little while Pepys went to the
waterside taking a boat to proceed up the
river. He comments on the rush of people

anxious to save their goods, and bringing them
to the bank till every boat no doubt was engaged.   All attempts to extinguish the flames
seemed a mockery ; for the high wind that was
blowing drove them on in an irresistible
manner, and carried flakes of fire a great
distance.   In the confusion domestic animals
must have fared badly; and there is a piteous
description of the poor pigeons, which many
people seem to have kept, dropping down into
the flames.   Unwilling to leave the houses, they
hovered about till their wings were burnt; and
then, of course, they were helpless.

Mr. Pepys was well-known at Court in consequence of his connection with naval affairs, and
he took the wise step of proceeding by water to
Whitehall and stating the urgency of the case to
some of the officials there.   The result was that
he had an interview with the King and the
Duke of York, in which he entreated the King
to give orders that certain houses should be
pulled down, as the only possible means of stopping the fire.   The King seemed much troubled—
as well he might be—and after some consultation

he commanded Mr. Pepys to go to the Lord Mayor from him, with instructions to spare no houses but to pull them down before the fire in every direction. The Duke of York added that if he wanted more soldiers to enforce his orders he should have them.

Then the diarist describes his return to the City: how he met with a friend who lent him his coach, in which he was driven as far as St. Paul's. There he got out, probably because further progress except on foot was impossible—for he says, " I walked along Watling Street as well as I could, every creature coming away loaded with goods to save, and here and there sick people carried away in beds. Extraordinary good goods carried in carts and on backs. At last met my Lord Mayor in Canning Street, like a man spent, with a handkercher about his neck." When Pepys gave him the King's orders he seemed quite overpowered and exclaimed, " What can I do ? I am spent ; people will not obey me. I have been pulling down houses ; but the fire overtakes us faster than we can do it."

The poor Lord Mayor was evidently at his

wit's end, and quite knocked up, for he had not been to bed all night; but it is to be hoped that he rallied sufficiently to go on with his duties. By this time people were filling the churches with their property, little suspecting how many of these massive structures would be consumed; but the fire still spread both east and west, and those who a few hours before had thought their dwellings secure from the flames began now to tremble, and in hot haste to remove their goods to any shelter they could find. In many cases furniture was removed twice if not three times, the place at first deemed safe being in a few hours in danger.

Later in the day Mr. Pepys was again on the river, where he met the King and the Duke of York in their barge, and proceeded with them to Queenhithe. The peremptory order still was to pull down houses as the only means of stopping the flames—the principle being just the same as that which dictates cutting away a tract of grass before the fire when in dry seasons the vast prairies of America take fire. When a great conflagration gets the mastery over ordi-

M

162 STORIES OF THE CITY OF LONDON.

nary endeavours to stay it there is nothing to be done save to deprive it of fuel.

We can, however, make allowance for people, many of whom were too ignorant to understand the necessity of the proceeding, when they showed reluctance to sacrifice houses as yet apparently safe, and I do not suppose it is possible in any description to exaggerate the horror and confusion which prevailed. Evelyn declares that many people were so overcome with misery and despair that they made hardly any efforts to lessen the calamity, but the generality, of course, struggled hard to save their property. Boats and barges were laden with goods, and it was remarked that nearly every house above the very meanest must have contained a pair of Virginells, so many were seen to be rescued. Virginells were a musical instrument, much used in the sixteenth and seventeenth centuries, of the nature of a spinet or harpsichord, but now quite superseded by the piano. It is pleasant to think that our ancestors had in so many instances the refining influence of music in their homes.

Mr. Pepys, whose house was in Axe Yard, the

very heart of the City, seems at first not to have
feared for his own premises, but the second day
of the fire he grew so alarmed that he began
removing his valuables; and we have a curious
picture of the times in his account of his bags
of gold, amounting to a good deal more than
£2,000, lying idle and hidden, and his vexation
at his wealth being seen. In those days the
necessaries of life were so much cheaper than
they are at present that Pepys' money-bags
really represented more wealth than is stated,
but we see it was not producing any interest.

By Monday, the 4th, it was computed there
were above ten thousand houses in flames, and
the heat was so terrible that no one could now
approach the conflagration. The flare of it was
seen for forty miles in all directions; and the
smoke was like a canopy that obscured the sky,
so that one writer describes travellers riding for
six miles at noonday beneath the shadow of it.
The fire now reached the Temple on the west
and Tower Street on the east, including, besides
Fenchurch Street and Gracechurch Street which
had been the earlier prey, Fleet Street, Ludgate

Hill, the Old Bailey, Newgate, Watling Street, Warwick Lane, Thames Street, and Billingsgate. A number of churches, as well as St. Paul's, were consumed. The Royal Exchange, as already mentioned, was destroyed, and the Rev. Thomas Vincent graphically describes a curious and impressive sight. He says—

" The sight of Guildhall was a fearful spectacle which stood the whole body of it together in view for several hours after the fire had taken it, without flames (I suppose because the timber was such solid oak) in a bright shining coal, as if it had been a palace of gold, or a great building of burnished brass."

It is, indeed, by no means very easy to combine in thought the roaring noise, the dazzling light, and burning heat experienced by the two hundred thousand people whom the calamity made homeless. The stones of St. Paul's are described as flying about like shot. From the bend of the river the fire naturally took the form of a bow, and Vincent, in a tract which he wrote called " God's Terrible Advice to the City by Plague and Fire," speaks of it as a dreadful bow "which had God's arrow in it with a flaming point." When we remember that the plague had raged only the previous year, and that it was yet breaking out occasionally in the suburbs, and that the country was in the midst of a war with the French and Dutch, we can understand in some degree the affliction of the nation.

By Tuesday, the 5th, the fire had reached Holborn and the entrance of Smithfield. But now the wind had lulled, and there was more hope of staying the progress of the flames. Instead of pulling down houses by mechanical means they were now blown up with gunpowder, "a measure," says Evelyn, "some stout seamen proposed early enough to have saved near the whole city; but this some tenacious and avaricious men, aldermen, &c., would not permit, because their houses must have been the first." At midday, on the 5th, the flames westward began to abate, and though towards Cripplegate the fire still burned fiercely; it gave way ultimately to the plan of blowing up houses before it. Of course, such a vast conflagration took many days to die out, and on the 7th,

Evelyn records the "extraordinary difficulty" of walking among the ruins and "clambering over heaps of yet smoking rubbish . . . the ground under my feet so hot that it even burnt the soles of my shoes."

Meanwhile the misery of the homeless multitude was very great. The King issued a proclamation for their relief, but they were too numerous to be properly housed, and they were glad of the shelter of tents and huts in the open country all round London. In the excitement and painful agitation of men's minds we cannot wonder that they listened to the idle tales which were circulated. The report spread that our enemies had set fire to the town, and were preparing to take advantage of the distress to land. However, they made no such attempt, and though the belief long prevailed that the Papists had occasioned the calamity there was no real foundation for the calumny.

Summing up the extent of the disaster, we have to record eighty-eight churches and thirteen thousand two hundred houses that were con-

sumed, the loss of property being estimated at
£7,385,000.

There is so much to regret in the character of
Charles the Second that it is pleasant to do him
justice when we can, and his conduct on the
occasion of the great fire seems to have been
admirable. He was on horseback or on foot for
many hours every day, giving orders for the
measures necessary to be taken, and forwarding
them by commands and example and threats,
and by the liberal distribution of money from
a hundred-pound bag which he carried with
him.

But dreadful as the calamity of the great fire
must have seemed at the time, God tempered it
with a hidden blessing. London that had often
been devasted by plague, and in the preceding
year in so marked and terrible a manner, has
never since been so afflicted. There is little
doubt that nothing short of fire could have
destroyed the germs of disease which hung about
the infected tenements, ready again to burst
out under often recurring conditions. In other
respects the City was unfavourable to health,

the streets being very narrow, and the generality of the houses crowded and incommodious.

There is something very gratifying to an English man or woman in reading of the energy displayed by the citizens at this period. " They beheld," says Sprat, " the ashes of their houses, gates, and temples without the least expression of pusillanimity. If philosophers had done this it had well become their profession of wisdom ; if gentlemen, the nobleness of their breeding and blood would have required it ; but that such greatness of heart should be found amongst the poor artizans and the obscure multitude is no doubt one of the most honourable events that ever happened."

Very few lives were lost in the fire, and this circumstance must have been looked on as a special mercy. Then another happy circumstance was that England had at hand the great archi- tect, Christopher Wren, who within three days of the fire submitted to the King his plan for rebuilding the City. Unfortunately, however, it was not carried out, for 'the selfishness and narrow-mindedness of individuals prevented

most of the improvements Wren had designed ;
but still the new London was a finer city than
the old, and much safer, in consequence of the
new houses being built of brick and stone
instead of wood.

Sir Christopher Wren—knighted a few years
after the fire—is perhaps best known as the
architect of our noble cathedral, St. Paul's ;
which, however, is still uncompleted. But he
built fifty-one other London churches, besides
numerous public buildings generally on the
sites of edifices which had been consumed by the
flames. He designed a monument to be erected
on the spot where the great fire broke out, but
the present structure is so different from that
he originally planned that it scarcely deserves to
be called his.

The popular opinion that the fire had been
the work of Popish incendiaries was so strong,
that when the Monument was first erected
it bore an inscription to the effect that the fire
had been caused by "the treachery and malice
of the Popish faction." When James the Second
came to the throne the words were erased ; but

unhappily the slander was restored and cut in
deep characters in the time of William the Third.
In the earlier part of the present century, however, the inscription was finally removed.   It
had always fostered ill-feelings; and it was to
that perpetuated falsehood that Pope alluded in
his famous couplet :—

> " Where London's column, pointing to the skies,
> Like a tall bully, lifts its head and lies."

Another great poet, Dryden, has described the
memorable fire of London with much force in
his poem "Annus Mirabilis," the " Year of Wonders." Alluding to the dismay of the citizens
roused from their slumbers, he says:—

> " Now streets grow throng'd and busy as the day;
>   Some run for buckets to the hallowed quire;
> Some cut the pipes, and some the engines play;
>   And some more bold mount ladders to the fire.
>
> In vain; for from the east a Belgian wind
>   His hostile breath through the dry rafters sent,
> The flames impell'd soon left their foes behind,
>   And forward with a wanton fury went.
>
> A quay of fire ran all along the shore,
>   And lighten'd all the river with a blaze;
> And waken'd tides began again to roar
>   And wondering fish in shining waters gaze.

Old Father Thames rais'd up his reverend head,
   But feared the fate of Simois would return : *
Deep in his ooze he sought his sedgy bed
   And shrunk his waters back into his urn.

The fire, meantime, walks in a broader gross,
   To either hand his wings he opens wide;
He wades the streets, and straight he reaches cross,
   And plays his longing flames on th' other side.

At first they warm, then scorch, and then they take;
   Now with long necks from side to side they feed;
At length grown strong their mother fire forsake,
   And a new colony of flames succeed.

To every nobler portion of the town
   The curling billows roll their restless tide,
In parties now they struggle up and down
   As armies unopposed for prey divide.

One mighty squadron with a side wind sped,
   Through narrow lanes his cumber'd fire does haste,
By powerful charms of gold and silver led
   The Lombard bankers and the 'Change to waste."

There are several more stanzas of the
"Annus Mirabilis" devoted to the description
of the fire of which no doubt Dryden was an

* That is, feared he would be dried up.

eye-witness. We owe much to poets who
put into vigorous language the thoughts of
the many. These may feel keenly though
they have not the power of expressing their
emotions.

THE GORDON RIOTS.

A.D. 1780.

LTHOUGH more than a century elapsed between the erection of the Monument with its slanderous inscription and the Riots of London in 1780, there was a certain continuity between the two events. The spirit of bitter animosity towards Papists had never slumbered among the nation at large, and now for many generations English Romanists had been looked on with aversion and distrust by the generality of their Protestant countrymen. Still there were a few tolerant and enlightened persons who lamented laws that perpetuated enmity and pressed heavily on a number of innocent families.

In the reign of William the Third a most severe law had been passed which restricted the liberty of Papists in a very cruel and arbitrary manner. It prohibited them from keeping schools, or taking upon themselves the education or government of youth in any other manner, under pain of perpetual imprisonment; it prevented them from inheriting property to which they were lawful heirs, and even from purchasing land; it made the very observance of their religious ceremonies difficult and hazardous. In point of fact, these laws were so shocking and unjust that they were constantly evaded; for only worthless people could be found to act as spies and informers. Still it was a dreadful thing for a man to be afraid of educating his children in his own faith, or to know that he was liable to be dispossessed of his rights, if the next heir chose to call himself a Protestant.

Among those who thought such restrictions cruel and unwise was a member of Parliament, Sir George Saville, who in 1778 brought in a

bill to repeal the harshest clauses in the Act of
William the Third. It was passed without
opposition, to the great satisfaction of all just
and liberal-minded people; but was looked on
very differently by the prejudiced and ignorant
masses.

In those days the masses were very ignorant,
a large proportion of the humbler classes not
being able to read or write. People of this sort
have, as a rule, only narrow sympathies and very
little reasoning power; as an old song says :—

> "Remember when the judgment's weak
> The prejudice is strong."

And when the very ignorant take up an idea in
an obstinate manner it is one of the hardest
things in the world to make them change it.

Now, a hundred years ago the generality of
people read very little; but probably they talked
among themselves a great deal. Stories of the
persecution of Protestants when the Roman
Catholics were in power had been handed down
from father to son for many generations, until
hatred of Popery was so widely spread that even
dull minds were fired with apprehension of evils

to come, should the English Roman Catholics be allowed liberty of action. This class were enraged at the passing of Sir George Saville's bill, which they denounced in the bitterest terms.

Meetings were held, at which no doubt the speakers fanned each other's fury, and angry pamphlets were circulated all over the country, the Scotch being the first to resort to violent measures. And yet Scotland was not included in Sir George Saville's bill; only had the Scotch Catholics been promised relief. As early as January, 1779, there were riots in Edinburgh, when the mob destroyed two Roman Catholic chapels, and a house where some priests lived. In Glasgow there was no chapel of the sort to denounce; but finding an earthenware manufacturer who was a Catholic they demolished his house and property, driving him and his family away with insult.

Meanwhile there was a member of Parliament, Lord George Gordon, who appears to have been one of those weak-minded men whom no amount of education could thoroughly enlighten. He was a brother of the Duke of Gordon, and had doubtless had all the advantages of education becoming his station; but now, at nine-and-twenty, he was as unreasoning a fanatic as many of the ignorant herd he was destined so fatally to influence.

Lord George Gordon had long been noted for his eccentric dress and strange behaviour, though up to this period he had probably been considered only a harmless oddity and nobody's enemy but his own. But that is rather a silly expression, for those weak and foolish people who are called "nobody's enemy but their own" often do a vast deal of mischief to others besides themselves. At an early age he had entered the Navy, but had left it in consequence of discontent, and an altercation about his promotion. After he obtained a seat in Parliament he distinguished himself by attacking all classes of politicians, sometimes, it must be owned, with a sort of cleverness; so that after a time the saying got about that there were three parties in the House, namely, the Ministers, the Opposition, and Lord George Gordon.

This was the man who denounced Sir George

N

Saville's bill of relief in the most violent and unreasonable manner. Soon he became the popular idol of the common people, his support greatly increasing the prevailing excitement. A Society was formed called the Protestant Association, of which he became the President, and to which so many persons subscribed that there was no lack of money to print and to aid the circulation of pamphlets, and get up petitions asking the repeal of Sir George Saville's bill. In the spring of 1780 Lord George presented several of these petitions to Parliament, he having at an earlier stage of the movement procured an interview with the King himself, in which he had urged, in fanatical language, the reimposing of pains and penalties on the Roman Catholics.

Probably because George the Third had given him no hope of royal assistance, he had the audacity to insinuate that the King was at heart a papist, and to declare in Parliament that the mass of the Scotch nation were of that opinion. It is rather surprising that at this stage of his proceedings he was not stopped in his course, for less disloyal words had often been counted treason; but it really appears that the members already looked upon him as a wild, unreasonable visionary, with whom it was waste of time to argue, and actually allowed themselves to be amused by his buffoonery. He talked of coming down to the House with a hundred and fifty thousand men at his back, and in the spring of 1780 he conceived the idea of a petition, the signatures to which should make it long enough to reach from the Speaker's chair to Whitehall.

At a meeting of the Protestant Association he announced his intention of presenting this petition on the 2nd of June, conditionally that the whole body of the Association and their friends should go in procession to present the petition; or, at any rate, that a number not less than twenty thousand should do so. Every one was to wear a blue cockade in his hat to distinguish him, and they were to meet in St. George's Fields.

On the 26th of May Lord George announced to the House of Commons that on the appointed day he should present the petition, accompanied by all those who had signed it. The signatures, however, in numerous instances, were only marks —that is, crosses affixed opposite the names, when the persons indicated were unable themselves to write. This circumstance may give an idea of the ignorance which prevailed among the mob of people who thought they were qualified to direct the legislation of their country!

According to Lord George Gordon's instructions, when Friday, June 2nd, arrived, a vast multitude assembled at the spot appointed. Their number has been variously estimated, but probably the crowd consisted of not less than sixty thousand men. They began to gather by ten o'clock in the morning, and marshalled themselves in ranks, waiting for their leader. "About eleven o'clock," says the "Annual Register," "Lord George arrived, and gave directions in what manner he would have them proceed, and about twelve, one party was ordered to go round over London Bridge, another over Blackfriars, and a third to follow him over Westminster." A roll of parchment, which was the petition, was borne before them, being carried on his head by a very tall man with a porter's knot, most probably to help him. They proceeded with perfect decorum six abreast, and the whole body reunited before the Houses of Parliament about half-past two o'clock, when they raised a great shout.

But however peaceably inclined many of the petitioners might be, the crowd had been joined on its way by not a few vagabonds and pickpockets, and a number of heedless youths who were only alive to the prospect of noisy excitement. It very soon became apparent that the unruly section was getting the upper hand. Not content with flaunting their own blue cockades and shouting "No Popery," they waylaid members of Parliament, and insisted on their wearing the cockades, and joining in the party cry.

The mob took possession of the avenues leading to the Houses of Parliament, and indeed twice attempted to force the doors. The Archbishop of York was insulted with groans and hisses and hootings. Lord Mansfield had the panels of his carriage beaten in, and narrowly escaped with life; Lord Bathurst, the President of the Council, was pushed about and kicked violently. The Duke of Northumberland was robbed of his watch, and the Bishop of Lincoln was so roughly treated that he probably owed his life to the circumstance of finding shelter in a house, where he changed his dress, and afterwards escaped over the leads of some neighbouring houses. The Bishop of Lichfield also had his gown rent.

The Lords Townshend and Hillborough were insulted, and so maltreated that, as the "Annual Register" says, they were "sent into the House without their bags and with their hair hanging loose on their shoulders." In those days gentlemen wore their hair very long and powdered; and the ends of the hair were gathered into a little black silk bag at the nape of the neck. Those who had not long hair wore artificial, and when you hear mention made of a "bag-wig," it is this style of wearing the hair which is meant. Long after it went out of fashion for general use, it remained a part of court dress; and quite as lately as fifty years ago, a few old

gentlemen were to be seen who had never relin-
quished the fashion of their youth, and constantly wore the " bag-wig." There are plenty
of pictures extant portraying it.

It would make a long list to enumerate the
various Peers who were maltreated by the mob.
Lord Stormont was in their hands for nearly half
an hour, being rescued at last by a gentleman
who addressed the rioters with some temporary
success; but no permanent impression was made,
and the crowd continued to behave more like
wild beasts than sane human creatures.

We can fancy what a scene must have presented itself inside the Houses of Parliament
when the members, with disordered hair and torn
clothes, and in many instances bearing even more
serious evidences of violence, at last forced their
entrance. All were in an angry and excited
state, all clamoured for something to be done,
though no one seemed clearly to know what
measures should be taken. Numbers were speaking at the same time, so that little could be
distinctly understood, especially as the hooting
and shouting outside were deafening.

Meanwhile Lord George Gordon must have added fuel to the fire instead of allaying it, by coming several times to the top of the gallery stairs and addressing the people, telling them of the bad treatment their petition was likely to meet with. Moreover, he mentioned several members who were opposed to it, especially Mr. Burke, the member for Bristol. He said, indeed, that there was some talk of the petition being taken into consideration on the following Tuesday, but that, for his own part, he did not like delays, as Parliament might be prorogued by that time. Afterwards he made a still more inflammatory speech, encouraging the idea that the King, dismayed by the numbers who were assembled, would himself interfere on their behalf.

General Conway and several other members warned him in strong language of the mischief he was doing by such harangues, and Colonel Gordon, a near relation, went up to him and addressed him in the following manner:—

"My Lord George, do you intend to bring your rascally adherents into the House of Com-

mons? If you do, the first man of them that
enters, I will plunge my sword, not into his, but
into your body."

While Lord George was making his second
speech another of his relations, General Grant,
came behind him and endeavoured to draw him
away, entreating him not to lead this mass of
people into danger. But his words did more
harm than good, for Lord George, instead of
answering him, proceeded to say, in addressing
the mob, " You see in this effort to persuade me
from my duty before your eyes an instance of
the difficulties I have to encounter from such
wise men of this world as my honourable friend
behind my back."

Alderman Sawbridge and some others now
tried to persuade the people to clear the lobby—
to which they had forced an entrance—but without success; and matters were so serious that
soon afterwards a party of Guards and Horse
arrived to enforce order. Justice Addington,
who appeared at the head of the troops, was
received with hisses, but on his assuring the
people that he would order the soldiers away if

only they would promise to disperse, he gained their good opinion. The cavalry galloped off, and about six hundred of the petitioners departed, but not till they had given three cheers for the magistrate.

When something like order was restored, Lord George introduced his petition, declaring it had nearly a hundred and twenty thousand signatures. After going through the necessary formalities, he moved that it should be taken into immediate consideration. After some debate the House divided, and there appeared six for the petition and a hundred and ninety-two against it. Soon afterwards the House broke up, the mob were presumed to disperse, and the Guards were ordered home.

But though order was restored in Westminster, the mob was by no means quieted. It divided into parties, one body marching to the Bavarian Roman Catholic Chapel, near Lincoln's Inn Fields, another to the Sardinian Chapel, in Warwick Street, Golden Square, both of which they almost entirely destroyed before the soldiers who were sent for could arrive. However, the rioters were in some measure quelled, thirteen of them being taken. It should be observed that both these chapels had been allowed to exist by treaties.

The next day, Saturday, affairs seemed less alarming; but on the afternoon of Sunday, the 4th, the rioters again assembled in great force, and proceeded, not only to attack the chapels, but the dwelling-houses of the Romanists in and about Moorfields. They stripped the chapels of all ornaments, and tore up altars, pews and pulpits to make bonfires of them, leaving nothing but the bare walls—and the houses they robbed of their furniture.

On the Monday the mob again collected, and paraded with some of their spoils to Lord George Gordon's house in Welbeck Street, evidently to show him what they had done, and afterwards burnt them in some fields near at hand. A hundred years ago Welbeck Street was on the outskirts of London, instead of being as now in the midst of the metropolis.

You may naturally wonder that the Government did not speedily put a stop to such out-

rageous proceedings, but it was not lawful
for the soldiers to fire on the people without the
authority of the civil magistrates, and the ceremony of reading the Riot Act of Parliament,
which justified using the military to quell disturbance of the peace; and probably for two
reasons the magistrates were slow to take violent
measures.   In the first place, they were anxious,
if possible, to avoid bloodshed; and, in the
next, it is not likely they forgot the fate of Mr.
Gillam, a magistrate who, only a dozen years
before, that is in 1768, had been tried for his
life because he gave orders to the soldiers to
fire on the crowd on the occasion of riots in St.
George's Fields.   He had borne with the rioters
for a long time, and the riot act had been twice
read before the firing, and it is hard to understand how he could have been even blamed.
But the remembrance of this circumstance must
have intimidated the magistrates in 1780.   It
is also probable that they did not yet perceive
the gravity of the occasion.   The soldiers were
called out, it is true, but, not being allowed to
defend themselves, they were absolutely insulted

and maltreated by the mob, the rioters pulling their noses and spitting in their faces.

Moreover, at a Cabinet Council held at St. James's this Monday morning, the Lord Chief Justice Mansfield had treated the riot as a comparatively trivial affair, and no decided measure had been taken except to offer a reward of five hundred pounds for the discovery of the rioters who had destroyed the Bavarian and Sardinian Chapels. Even when, later in the day, Strahan the printer called on him to express his apprehensions, and no doubt to describe much that was happening, he could not be made to see the affair in its true light. Little could the Chief Justice have imagined the victim he himself was speedily to be.

Doubtless many other people were of Lord Mansfield's opinion, and thought that surely now the tumult would subside; otherwise we cannot fancy they would have had the heart to go through the ceremony of attending the drawing-room, however loyal they might have felt. With London in the hands of the rabble, the state and pageantry of the Court seemed out of place. But the 4th of June was the King's birthday, and falling on a Sunday it was kept in the usual manner on the following day. George the Third was, at that time especially, a much-beloved king, and his birthday was always kept as a festival. As was usual, he held a drawing-room, and an ode written by the Poet Laureate was chanted in his honour. But while the carriages and sedan-chairs of the nobility were taking them to Court, the "blue cockades" were busy doing infinite mischief in other parts of the town. They wreaked their vengeance on some tradesmen who had given evidence against the rioters that were committed to Newgate by plundering their shops; and a detachment of the mob made its way to Leicester Fields to attack the house of Sir George Saville, the author of the bill for the relief of the Papists This they stripped of its furniture and then set fire to the building.

On the morning of Tuesday the 6th both Houses of Parliament met. A detachment of foot-guards was placed in Westminster Hall;

but the mob, well aware that they would not fire
without the riot act being read, waylaid the
Peers and Commoners, and insulted and maltreated them just as they had done on the
Friday. They dragged Lord Sandwich from
his carriage, which they demolished, and ill-
treated him, though he was rescued by a Justice
of the Peace, who appeared with a party of soldiers. Mr. Hyde, the Justice, rode among the
crowd with the cavalry, hoping to disperse the
offenders; but the soldiers were so fearful of
exceeding the law that they would not even
strike the mob with the flat of their swords.
One almost fears that the soldiers—who were
for the most part far more ignorant than
the soldiers of the present day—must have
sympathized in some measure with the rioters.

Mr. Hyde paid dearly for his generous and
patriotic conduct, for the mob raised the cry of
"To Hyde's house, ahoy!" and proceeding to
St. Martin's Lane, where he lived, they speedily
pulled down his house.

There was great indignation in the House of
Commons when Lord George appeared wearing

the hateful blue cockade.   One member, indeed,
Colonel Herbert, declared his resolve not to sit
and vote in the House while the noble Lord wore
the ensign of riot in his hat, and vowed that if
his lordship did not remove it he would do it
for him.   Lord George seemed cowed by this
threat, for he took the cockade from his hat and
put it in his pocket.   No doubt by this time he
was alarmed at the turn affairs had taken, and
began to perceive that they had passed quite
beyond his control.   He had issued a hand-bill
on the part of the Protestant Association dis-
avowing any share in the riots, but it made no
impression on the mob.

The orator Edmund Burke and Sir George
Saville seemed to have the clearest heads in the
House of Commons.   They recommended all
parties to unite and persuade ministers to take
strong measures; but the majority of members
appeared frightened, and carried a resolution to
the effect that the famous petition should be
taken into consideration when the disorders had
subsided.   There was some talk of committing
Lord George to the Tower, but whilst this

measure was under discussion there was alarming news from the city, and the House adjourned in a hurry.

The mob was now more dangerous and ungovernable than ever. The more respectable members of the Protestant Association, however fanatical their opinions might be, were not thieves nor despoilers, and in consternation at the destruction which had taken place, had withdrawn from the scene. They were frightened at the disturbance, though they could not have been ignorant that they had helped to occasion it. The rioters now consisted mainly of pickpockets and burglars, and the vilest dregs of the populace—wretched beings without conscience and for the most part as ignorant as savages; though it is to be feared there were not a few youths who were led to take part in the work of destruction from a mere unreasoning love of excitement.

While the House of Commons was sitting the rioters attacked the house of the Prime Minister, Lord North, but happily some soldiers succeeded in saving the mansion. Foiled in this attempt the mob now marched on to Newgate, vowing they would break open the prison and release their fellows who had been imprisoned there since Friday. They were armed with crow-bars and pickaxes and heavy sledge hammers, and on the governor refusing to give up their comrades they attacked his door and windows and when these gave way flung the furniture out of the window and set fire to his dwelling by throwing fire-brands and combustibles into it. While it was burning they attacked the strong door of the prison with their tools; but finding it did not yield they brought heaps of the governor's furniture which they piled against the door and then set on fire.

From the governor's house the flames spread to the prison chapel, and thence to some passages leading to the wards. On perceiving this the mob raised shouts and yells of triumph, which were mingled with shouts and cries from the prisoners, some of whom were delighting in the expectation of release, while others were dreading that they should perish by fire. The rioters had broken into the governor's cellar and were maddening themselves with wine and spirits till their ferocity knew no bounds.

Many of the mob had themselves at one time or another been prisoners in Newgate, and were well acquainted with its interior, and led on by them the crowd made a rush through the gaps caused by the fire, and soon found themselves masters of the place. Three hundred criminals, four of whom were under sentence of death, were thus released—not one being left behind, and not one perishing in the flames. They joined the roaring multitude, and shouted their rejoicing at seeing the new strong prison consumed by fire. Newgate prison had been lately rebuilt at a vast expense, but by the next morning, nothing remained of it but the blackened walls.

When we consider the severity of the English laws a century ago, when men were hanged for petty thefts and offences, that now are only punished by a short imprisonment, it seems probable that the released criminals were not any viler than the mob they joined, but at any rate they added to its number. Even in the case of the four men under sentence of death, it by no

means follows that they were murderers or culprits of the deepest dye. And it is told that one
of them when the riots were quelled gave himself up again to justice. One feels curious to
know whether he was so weary of life that he was
willing to resign it, or whether he foresaw that
he should be pardoned, as speedily was the case.

After burning Newgate the next proceeding
of the mob was to break open Clerkenwell prison
and release the prisoners there, who of course
swelled the crowd. Aided by this reinforcement
they attacked the houses of two very active
magistrates, Mr. Cox and Sir John Fielding, and
then with increasing fury proceeded to Bloomsbury Square, where Lord Mansfield resided.
Already, they felt themselves so completely masters of London, that they compelled the terrified citizens to illuminate their houses and hang
out flags and banners with the inscription, "No
Popery," upon them. Even the Jews wrote on
their doors, "This house is Protestant." Business
was almost entirely suspended, shops with few
exceptions being closed from Tyburn to White-
chapel; and the more courageous people armed

themselves with whatever weapons they could command. Many houses looked like places prepared for a siege.

A friend narrates that two of his grand parents were married in London during the week of the Gordon Riots. When all arrangements are made, and guests invited, it is troublesome to put off a wedding; thus the ceremony was duly performed, notwithstanding the terrible state of the town. It would, however, have been impossible after leaving the church to pass with safety through the streets, in only the ordinary manner; so the wedding party assumed the blue cockades instead of white favours, and covered the post chaise containing the bridal pair with placards of "No Popery." Thus in the guise of violent partizans did they escape into the country.

Lord Mansfield, the Lord Chief Justice of England, was one of the ablest and most conscientious men ever raised to his exalted position. He was emphatically a "just judge," and it was because he had administered the law impartially to churchmen and dissenters, to quakers and to Roman Catholics; and especially because he had refused to convict a priest for exercising the offices of his religion that the mob were incensed against him.

It was about midnight when the rioters, infuriated with spirits and beer—which they had extorted from publicans—arrived at Lord Mansfield's house in Bloomsbury Square, which was then a fashionable part of London. Of course, a private residence could offer but little resistance to the attacks of such a multitude, and Lord Mansfield, now seventy-five years of age, and Lady Mansfield had barely time to escape by a back-door before the mob effected an entrance by demolishing the doors and windows. Then they proceeded to throw out the furniture, pictures and books, which were speedily made into bonfires.

Lord Mansfield had one of the finest libraries in England, and its destruction by an ignorant rabble, who were quite incapable of estimating its value may be justly considered as a national loss. It had been the collection of a long life, and comprised not only law books but valuable works of general literature. And besides the books many important papers and deeds were consumed, and a vast collection of letters from eminent men which Lord Mansfield was said to have preserved to aid him in writing the memoirs of his own times, a task which he had hoped to perform. When furniture, pictures, wearing apparel, books, and papers were consumed, the mob set fire to the house, having first broken into the wine cellar and added to their intoxication by drinking the fine wines they found there.

It is a most surprising fact that early in these savage proceedings, though a party of foot guards appeared on the scene, they remained quite inactive; and when a friend of Lord Mansfield's remonstrated with them they declared that without the orders of a magistrate they dared not act, and that the magistrates had all fled from the scene in terror! Imagine what it must have been to witness the wholesale destruction of property that was taking place by a party of ferocious ruffians armed with sledge-hammers, iron bars and many other formidable weapons; while combustibles were kindled in all the rooms ; and at the same time a party of soldiers with muskets in their hands looking calmly on awaiting the necessary order to quiet the tumult ! Certainly some one in authority must have been greatly and gravely to blame. When at last a magistrate was found and the soldiers were ordered to fire, the work of destruction was done, and probably the men who were killed and wounded were so stupefied with drink that they were hardly conscious of the retribution. The whole story of these riots is a very painful one. An ignorant and vicious rabble, powerful only from their brute strength, were in reality masters of London for several days, while the class who should have controlled them seemed paralyzed by fear.

On Wednesday the 7th, the consternation of well-disposed people seemed at its height. They barricaded their houses, chalked " No Popery " on their doors, and hung out blue streamers— blue being the colour of the Protestant Association. But protestant zeal had now nothing to do with the mob, which was only bent on plunder and destruction. Some of the rioters were

armed with iron bars which had been the rail-
ings in front of Lord Mansfield's house, and
they went about stripping the houses tenanted
by quiet respectable people, or levying contribu-
tions of money from them. One man who rode
on horseback claimed gold and would take
nothing less.

Not satisfied with having destroyed Lord
Mansfield's town house a party of rioters proceeded to his residence near Highgate, intending
to burn that also, but happily they were met by
a detachment of cavalry who turned them back.
They had also intended to sack the Bank of
England, but found it guarded by infantry, who
fired on them, killing and wounding a great
number. They were however apparently but
little daunted, for they broke open several prisons,
including the King's Bench, the Fleet and the
Marshalsea, of course setting free the prisoners.
They plundered the toll-houses at Blackfriars
Bridge and then burnt them down, and had so
systematized their proceedings that they had a
list of the public buildings they intended to
destroy, the Mansion House, the Royal Ex-

change and the British Museum being among them. Happily their plans were frustrated with regard to these buildings. They even threatened to break open Bedlam and release its miserable and dangerous inmates.

One more dreadful scene, however, had yet to be enacted. Mr. Langdale, who had a large distillery on Holborn Bridge was a Roman Catholic. Probably his stores of spirits were the temptation to violence, though his religion was made the excuse for it. The rioters broke open his premises, staved in his hogsheads of spirits, filled pails and even their hats with the liquor, drank deeply of it, and passed it on to the mob outside till the kennels ran with gin and brandy and pure alcohol; and even wretched women and children, as well as men, were seen on their knees sucking up the intoxicating fluid. Some of these miserable beings, helpless from drunkenness, perished in the flames, for as usual the plundered premises were set on fire and, flooded as they were by the spirit that was spilt, the flames at once sprang up high and spread in all directions.

It was about this time that, as Dr. Johnson recorded, there were thirty-six fires burning at the same time. Happily it was calm summer weather, for had the wind been high the flames must have spread, and the historian would probably have had to record another great fire of London.

Meanwhile the timidity and irresolution of the Government had been disastrous. It was said that the Ministers even stooped to curry favour with the mob by allowing their servants to flaunt the blue cockade. But on this Wednesday the 7th, the Government seemed to imbibe vigour. It is greatly to the credit of George the Third that he showed much more courage and determination than his Ministers on this occasion. He called a council at which he presided, and asked what steps the Government was going to take to suppress the frightful tumult. The whole Cabinet appeared confused at the question, and instead of answering it promptly, begged leave to remind the King of the verdicts which had been passed against officers who discharged military duties against the rioters in 1768. It was the prevailing opinion that it was not lawful to attack the mob, whatever it might do, until an hour after reading the Riot Act. This was quite a perversion of the meaning of the Act, but even had such belief been well founded, it was no excuse for the recent neglect, for officers were ready to perform their duty at command, and had sat for hours on their horses surrounded by troops, watching the wild excesses of the mob and the destruction of property, but waiting for authority to fire.

Wedderburn, the Attorney-General, afterwards Lord Loughborough, was the first to answer the King's question in a satisfactory manner. He declared that not a single hour after reading the Act was required for the dispersion of the mob, and that in such extreme cases as so many recent ones had been not even the reading of the Act was necessary if a military force was required to prevent the firing of a dwelling-house—the act being felony.

Encouraged by this high legal decision, the King declared it had always been his opinion that such was the law and that now he would act with decision. There should, he said, be at least one magistrate in the kingdom who would do his duty. The opinion of the Attorney-General and the firmness of the King seemed to give the council courage. A proclamation was issued requiring all householders and their families to keep within doors, while the King's officers suppressed the riot by military force.

This proclamation was speedily followed by the despatch of soldiers to various quarters of the town. Now began scenes only less horrible than the preceding ones. The first body of troops called into operation was the Northumberland militia, who had entered London by a forced march only that day. They were led against the rioters at Langdale's distillery, where already there had been great loss of life. Another party proceeded to Blackfriars Bridge, where numbers perished by falling from the parapet into the river. Other troops marched off to other districts to restore order, and whenever the mob failed to disperse the word of command was given and the troops fired in volleys.

Remembering how narrow many of the London streets then were it is easy to understand that many of the crowd might be eager to escape and yet could not do so. But on the other hand time had been allowed for well-disposed persons to remain at home, and those who failed to obey suffered the dreadful consequences. It must indeed have been horrible for quiet citizens who had obeyed the proclamation to remain in their closed houses with shutters barred to listen to the tramp of soldiers, the hooting of the crowd, and the firing of muskets with military precision, followed by the shrieks of the wounded. But the five days of terror through which they had passed must have made them deeply thankful that the Government was defending them at last, and in many instances bodies of civilians armed themselves and came forth to assist the troops.

Not less than twenty-five thousand soldiers were now assembled in London and the suburbs, all ready to act as occasion might require, and this display of force, together with the energy of the authorities, now thoroughly aroused, so quelled the turbulent mass that by night the town was perfectly quiet. The streets indeed seemed even more still than usual, for wearied with the recent excitement people were thankful to rest. In many places blood ran in the kennels, for it was computed that two hundred men were shot in the streets, and two hundred and fifty were carried to the hospitals seriously wounded, of whom subsequently nearly a hundred died. Of course there must have been many more slightly injured who managed to escape.

On the next morning, Thursday the 8th of June, it has been said " the city looked in places as if it had been sacked by an invading army." Firemen were busy among the smoking ruins of prisons and other buildings trying to extinguish the still smouldering remains; while men and women—the latter often with children in their arms—were lying about on doorsteps and on bulks and stalls sleeping off the fumes of the previous day's drunkenness. Troops were stationed in the parks, at the Royal Exchange and some other important places, but most of the shops still continued closed, and no public business was transacted except at the Bank of England.

On the morning of Friday the 9th the law courts resumed their sittings, and shops once more were generally opened. On this day Lord George Gordon, the author of all the disasters, was committed to the Tower on a Secretary of State's warrant. When he was arrested at his house in Welbeck Street he made no resistance, only observing to the officers, " If you are sure it is I you want, I am ready to attend you." He was charged with high treason, and a strong guard escorted him to that famous stronghold. Perhaps it had been thought that there would be some attempt to rescue him, but his adherents were now quite subdued, and as spiritless as himself.

When the Parliament met on the 19th—for it had been adjourned during the riot—the King delivered a speech, in which he justified the measures he had taken to suppress the disturbance. But no one thought such justification necessary; people only lamented that military force had not been employed earlier. Addresses were moved in each house thanking the King for his paternal care of the public interest, and they were warmly carried, for the King had been the first to see the exigence of the case and to act with the needful spirit.

It is surprising that any sensible person could have been found who disapproved of the manner in which the riots had at last been put down; but there must have been some dissentient opinion, or Lord Mansfield would not have thought it necessary in the House of Peers to defend the employment of the military as he did. In speaking of the legality of the measure he made an allusion to the loss of his library which must have been pathetic.

" I have not," he said, "consulted books, indeed I have no books to consult. His Majesty and those who have advised him, I repeat it, have acted in strict conformity to the common law. The military have been called in, and very wisely called in—not as soldiers, but as citizens. No matter whether their coats be red or brown, they were employed, not to subvert but to preserve the laws and constitution which we all so highly prize."

This famous speech has become an authority

P

on the question of the legality of employing soldiers to suppress a riot. It expresses the simple law on the subject. Soldiers are to be employed where civil authority fails, but only under civil authority. When a mob begins to destroy property the act becomes felony, and a magistrate is justified in reading the Riot Act, and if the crowd does not instantly disperse, in ordering the military to fire upon it.

The day after the assembling of Parliament the Commons entered into consideration of the great Protestant petition, and very strong was the discussion which ensued. The outcome of it, however, was that the cruel restrictions on the Roman Catholics were not re-enacted.

In the course of a few weeks rioters to the number of one hundred and thirty-five were tried—several of them being women. Those who had been imprisoned in the city were tried at the regular Old Bailey sessions; the others on the Surrey side of the river by a royal commission. About one half were found guilty; and of those thus convicted twenty-one were executed and the remainder transported for life.

Among those sentenced to death was Edward
Dennis, the common hangman, who however for
some reason or another was reprieved. The
trial of Lord George Gordon was postponed until the beginning of the following year.

It is dreadful to reflect on the ignominious
death of so many wretched people, among whom
were women, but it is also dreadful to picture
to ourselves the scenes of terror and destruction
for which the culprits suffered. Their trials
were conducted with calmness and decorum,
and according to the law of England, as it then
existed, by their theft and violence and especially by their setting fire to buildings they had
incurred the penalty of death. It is computed
that seventy-two private houses were consumed
by fire, besides the four gaols, during this week
of terror.

When an estimate was made of the loss sus-
tained, both Lord Mansfield and Sir George
Saville declined to accept compensation for the
destruction of their valuable property.

The trial of Lord George Gordon took place
on February 5th, 1781. He was arraigned for

high treason as "George Gordon Esq commonly called Lord George Gordon," because he was a commoner not a peer, the title by which he was known being what is called a courtesy title accorded to him as the son of a duke. The prisoner was defended with great eloquence by Mr., afterwards Lord, Erskine, and the presiding judge was William Earl of Mansfield, who had been so wronged by the rioters.

But it was in keeping with Lord Mansfield's greatness of character that he allowed no personal enmity to appear on this memorable occasion. On the contrary, in his charge to the jury he dwelt so forcibly on all the points of law that were in the prisoner's favour, and summed up the evidence so clearly, that the jury after half an hour's deliberation pronounced the prisoner *"not guilty."*

No doubt this verdict disappointed many of those people who were still smarting under the remembrance of all they had suffered during the riots, and who believed quite truly that Lord George had been the original instigator of the disturbance. But technically the lawyers were right in their expounding of the law. His presenting the petition was not illegal, and however morally he was responsible for what followed he was not so legally.

Perhaps the worst point against him was the fact of his having given letters of protection to certain persons worded in the following manner :—

" All true friends to Protestants will be particular, and do no injury to the property of any true Protestant, as I am well assured the proprietor of this house is a staunch and worthy friend to the cause.

"G. GORDON."

This certainly was very like giving the authority of a leader to injure those who were not Protestants.

However he was not without sympathizers, for some persons thought he had been made the scape-goat of the magistrates, who by neglecting their duty had allowed the rioters to proceed in their depredations instead of suppressing the tumult at an early stage.

As years passed on the eccentricities of Lord George Gordon increased, and the wonder is that his family did not put him under restraint. In 1786, he was excommunicated by the Archbishop of Canterbury for his refusal to appear as a witness in an ecclesiastical court, the sentence being pronounced in the church of St. Mary-le-bonne, on the 7th of April in that year.

In 1788 he was tried and found guilty of libelling the Queen of France, the French Ambassador and the English law and crown officers. On this he withdrew to Holland, but the magistrates of Amsterdam sent him back to England. He was committed to Newgate in accordance with the sentence pronounced on him for libel, and there spent the short remainder of his life. He died of fever, November the 1st, 1793.

Some years previously he had changed his religion, giving up the Christian faith, notwithstanding his former zeal for the Protestant cause. Chroniclers of the time say he became a Jew; and conformed strictly to all the Jewish observances. This he might do, but the Jews are a nation, a race, a peculiar people, and in reality no "gentile" can become one of them. The circumstance, however, is but another proof of a certain weakness of mind, so nearly allied to insanity, that one is inclined to close the history of Lord George Gordon with more of pity than censure. But the riots which still bear his name taught a terrible lesson, showing how fearful a thing it is for ignorant brute force, excited by angry and unreasoning passion, to get the upper hand even for an hour.

THE THAMES TUNNEL.

WITH PERSONAL RECOLLECTIONS OF THE ENGINEER.

IT cannot be quite easy for young persons of the present day to imagine the London of fifty or sixty years ago, and the manner of life its citizens led; for to do so requires nearly as much mental effort as is necessary to realize the descriptions of far more distant times. At the period when Marc Isambard Brunel conceived the idea of the Thames Tunnel, there was no such thing as railway travelling; no uniform penny postage, and a score of conveniences now in general use were then unknown. Above all, the mighty engineering works which within the last half century have become new wonders of the world had no existence. It is necessary to understand and remember all this, when considering the genius and character of a man who was in many respects even more interesting than his works.

Marc Isambard Brunel was by birth a Frenchman, having been born at the village of Hocqueville in Normandy, April 25th, 1769. His father was a small landed proprietor, and, with something of the ambition which in many other countries is felt by the same class, he originally intended his son for the church. But the youth had no predilection for a clerical career, while he very early evinced remarkable talent for all sorts of mechanical contrivances. In fact he was only happy carpentering and constructing. There seems to have been no thought of indulging him entirely in the choice of a profession—but a sort of compromise was effected. The father gave up the cherished idea of his son becoming a priest, and the son consented to enter the French Navy.

To qualify himself for the service, he studied mathematics, in which he made astonishing progress in a short space of time. It is said that he never required to read a proposition in Euclid more than once; and when he was introduced to the naval officer under whom he was about to serve, it was an opportunity for proving his powers of observation and memory.

There happened to be a quadrant on the table, and though from his reading he was acquainted with the nature of the instrument, he had never seen one before; he did not dare to touch it, but by walking round the table and carefully looking at it, he was able to construct an instrument which he used all the time he was in the Navy. He was by this time accomplished in both drawing and penmanship; the latter as executed by him was—to use a common expression—like a copper-plate engraving in its neatness and precision. It was not by any means small writing, and least of all was it like the ordinary writing of the French; beautiful it was to look at, with a peculiar character of its own and as easy to read as print. As it became his habit to give written instructions to those who were employed by him in his great achievements this rare handwriting was a great advantage.

His accomplishment in drawing may be estimated by the fact that he could draw an exact circle with his hand, and then determine the centre of it with perfect precision. Only a very few great artists have been able to do this.

Brunel, however, was not destined to remain long in the Navy. The Great French Revolution broke out, and all who belonged to the better classes were more or less in danger. Brunel was in the Royal Navy, and was besides just well enough born to be called an "aristocrat." Happening to be in Paris at the time that the revolutionary assembly voted the death of the unfortunate Louis the Sixteenth, he became a marked man in consequence of a few words he uttered at a *café*. They were expressive, of strong condemnation of the proceedings of the Assembly; and to make matters worse he was heard to call to his dog in derision as a "citizen." It was just at the time when all titles were abolished, and the noblest in the land, and the lowest and most ignorant were alike called " citizens." Brunel's defence of the unhappy King and his " *viens citoyen !* " to his dog nearly brought him to the guillotine.

At this time Brunel was in his twenty-fourth year and engaged to be married to a young English lady—Miss Sophia Kingdom—whose acquaintance he had made while she was at school at Rouen. I, who am telling you this story, knew them both in their old age, and have heard them speak with much emotion of that troubled time. Brunel managed to escape to America—doubtless in full confidence that Miss Kingdom being English would be safe. Such, however, was not the case. Her engagement to the proscribed man compromised her, and it was several months before her friends could rescue her. Girl as she was she was confined in a prison, and always believed that she owed her release at last to the pity of the jailor's wife.

During the voyage to America, Brunel made the acquaintance of a gentleman who was engaged to make certain surveys in connection

with the Hudson, and gladly accepted from him
the situation of his assistant. In this employment Brunel so distinguished himself that on
his return to New York he was very soon
engaged as engineer in the construction of
various sorts of machinery, and as architect in
the erection of public buildings. He made improvements in the printing press, and in the
machinery for the boring of ordnance. The
first theatre at New York was built after his
designs; it was subsequently burned down but
is said to have been famous for its symmetry
and beauty.

In this manner seven years passed away.
Great and dreadful events had happened in
France, and Brunel had no desire to return to
his own .country, then passing under the sway
of Bonaparte. But he did desire to make Miss
Kingdom his wife, and to find in her country
his home. Indeed he had long felt enthusiasm
about England, for it is related of him that
when a schoolboy he was lost in admiration of
her manufacturing skill. His chief recreation
at Rouen was watching the ships at the quays.

One day some large iron castings were landed, which seemed to take him by surprise. He found, in answer to his inquiries, that they were parts of an engine to pump by steam and were intended for the Paris waterworks. "England —England!" cried the boy, "what a country it must be to make such machines as these! I must see it when I am a man."

Accordingly his boyish wish was gratified; he left America, and arrived in England in the year 1800. The reputation of his talents had preceded him, and henceforth they were devoted to his adopted country as energetically as if he had been truly her son. The betrothed pair were so aged and altered by the trials they had encountered that neither would have known the other had they met as strangers. This they said when telling of those old times forty years afterwards.

Brunel's first great invention by which England profited, was that for improvement in the machinery for making blocks for the Navy. Many difficulties had to be surmounted, and the rights of a patent to be respected, so that it was not

until the year 1808 that his machinery came
into full operation. By it six men can do the
work of sixty under the old method; and his
invention was the origin of many mechanical
improvements that save labour.

Brunel's block machinery at once saved the
government £20,000 per annum, and he asked
that sum as his reward. It was not accorded;
two thirds of a year's saving having been the
award. His reputation however as a first class
engineer was now established, and works of
great importance succeeded each other with
rapidity. The first double-acting marine steam
engine was his invention.

But the project into which perhaps more than
all others he threw his best energies was that of
connecting the northern and southern banks of
the Thames below Bridge in such a manner that
navigation would not be impeded; and this
could only be done by means of a tunnel.

Now before we can rightly estimate Brunel's
genius and work we have to remember that the
idea of the Thames Tunnel, had been in his
mind for many years before he could find a suffi-

cient number of persons with faith in him to provide the necessary funds for his undertaking, and so form a Company. Perhaps we ought not to wonder at the public being slow to believe in the possibility of such a work being completed; for there had been much talk of a similar thing at the close of the last century, when it had been pronounced impracticable by a skilful engineer. Notwithstanding this opinion, something of the sort had been attempted a few years later, but after considerable labour the work had been abandoned—which failure of course only confirmed belief in the engineer's opinion.

But though Brunel believed that he should accomplish his object, he in no way underrated the difficulties he should have to encounter. The greatest of these unquestionably was the nature of the soil which forms the bed of the Thames. Geologists knew that beyond a particular depth a sort of quicksand would be reached; it was therefore necessary to keep well above so insecure a foundation. In fact the nearer to the bottom of the river the tunnel could be made the stronger it would be, besides the advantage of the road-way to it being the less steep.

It was early in the year 1824 that the Thames Tunnel Company was formed, and the work actually commenced. This was done by sinking a shaft at Rotherhithe, on the Surrey side of the river. This gigantic shaft was built up on the spot where it was desired it should sink. At a hundred and fifty feet distant from the river the bricklayers built up a round frame three feet thick and a hundred and fifty feet in circumference. This was strengthened by iron rods passing up the centre of the thickness, and was raised in the first instance to the height of forty-two feet. Then workmen began to excavate from the inside, the earth being raised to the top of the shaft by steam power. Of course when sufficient earth had been removed the masonry began to sink into the ground, and we can imagine the gradual descent of this mighty structure to have been a really grand sight. As however one tier was lost to view, another was added to the top, until the shaft was sixty-five feet in height.

Q

By means of a smaller shaft the workmen bored to eighty feet, but at that depth the ground suddenly gave way, while sand and water were blown up violently. This proved the truth of the geologists' statement. It was at the depth of sixty-three feet from the surface that the Tunnel was commenced.

Meanwhile there had been constructed the shield on which Brunel relied for his success. Like many other great men he was a keen observer, and never disdained a lesson from the simple operations of nature. He had noticed the manner in which the teredo, or ship-worm, did the mischief which caused it to be named by Linnæus *Calamitas navium*. This little creature can gnaw through the hardest wood, but is itself protected by an entire shell. "He has his shield," said Brunel, "and I will have mine."

Brunel's shield was a huge fabric of iron, which was pushed forward six inches at a time, and supported the bed of the river while the workmen undermined it. The shield consisted of twelve divisions, each containing three cells—the alternate divisions being one a little before the other. The entire front was defended by boards, called "poling boards," which could be moved one at a time. The men began by pulling down the top poling board, and excavating for six inches. They then replaced the board and removed the next in order, and cut away the earth in like manner until the entire space in front of the shield was cleared. By means of screw machinery the shield was then pushed forward, and the operation of beginning at the top poling board, and cutting away six inches was repeated.

As the shield advanced, supporting the bed of the river, men worked diligently in its rear, forming the strong brick walls of the top, sides, and bottom, the shield still holding up the earth overhead. The tunnel formed a double archway, each archway being fifteen feet high and wide enough for a single carriage-way and footpath. But the brickwork was so thick that the excavation required was twenty-two and a half feet high and thirty-eight feet broad. Following the shield was a stage in each archway for the convenience of the men in the upper cells.

Sinking the shaft, however, and making necessary preparations for the most difficult part of the work took so much time that it was not till January, 1826, that the Tunnel itself was really commenced. The first nine feet showed only firm clay, but then the workmen came to watery sand which made all progress difficult, and but for many precautions dangerous. There were thirty-two days of great anxiety, but by the middle of March substantial soil was again reached, and the work went on very steadily until September, when two hundred and sixty-feet of the tunnel had been completed.

On the 14th of that month Brunel terrified the Directors by informing them that he expected the river would break in with the next tide. He had discovered a cavity above the top of the shield. His prediction was exactly fulfilled, but so admirable had been the precautions taken that no harm was done. A few weeks later a similar accident occurred; and on the 2nd of January, 1827, during the removal of one of the poling boards, the tide forced a quantity of loose clay through the shield. Still there was not much mischief done, and no irruption of the river followed. By this time three hundred and fifty feet were accomplished, and the work went on satisfactorily for the next three months, although the ground was suspiciously moist.

In April it was found desirable to examine the bed of the river by means of a diving-bell, and some depressions were found and filled up with bags of clay. On this occasion a shovel and hammer were accidentally left in the river, and some time afterwards, during an influx of loose earth through the shield, were recovered, they having sunk eighteen feet. This circumstance may give some idea of the watery unstable nature of the soil through which the shield had to force its way, the workmen making all water-tight as they proceeded. But a greater calamity than any yet experienced was now near at hand.

About the middle of May some vessels were moored just above the Tunnel, and the obstruction they occasioned caused a great washing away of the soil beneath them. On the 18th of this month there was such a great and sudden influx of sand and water that several of the men in the Tunnel barely escaped with life. The water and sludge rushed through in such overwhelming volumes that the stream was soon up to their waists, while the sudden rush of air, or else the water, extinguished all the lights. Left in perfect darkness and with a roar of waters so deafening that they could scarcely hear one another speak it is marvellous that they ever reached the stairway of the shaft.

The fear was that the staircase would blow up, and Mr. I. K. Brunel, the engineer's son and valuable assistant, ordered the men to use all expedition; nor were they a moment too soon, for hardly had they reached the second flight of stairs, when the first which they had just mounted gave way. Indeed one poor man was still struggling in the water, but Mr. I. K. Brunel, young and active, with great presence of mind slid down one of the iron ties, and with the assistance of Mr. Gravett, who followed his example, fastened a rope round the man's waist and he was soon drawn out of danger. When the roll was called happily not one was missing.

The diving-bell was now again used, and the hole in the bed of the river discovered. Three thousand bags of clay, and a number of small hazel rods were used to close the chasm and a lighter loaded with old iron was sunk above them, but it was not till the 21st of the next month that the water which had rushed into the Tunnel was got under, and not till the middle of August that the soil was sufficiently cleared away for the engineer to examine thoroughly the effects of the disaster. The structure of the Tunnel was found quite sound, though the shield and some of the brickwork showed the violence of the rush of water.

The work was now recommenced; but its difficulties increased rather than diminished. The farther the men proceeded the more foul the air became, so that it was no uncommon thing for the labourers to be seized with sudden illness and brought to the upper world in a state of insensibility. To their honour however be it said, that for the most part they felt enthusiasm in their work, and devotion to Brunel, whom they found a kind and considerate master. They seemed to have a share in the glory of the undertaking and by all accounts worked with a will.

By the beginning of the year 1828 the middle of the river was reached; the men, working in relays day and night made rapid progress, but a terrible disaster was now near at hand. At six o'clock in the morning of January 12th there was the usual change of men and the fresh gang began to work in their customary manner. Suddenly, when they had only proceeded about a foot downwards, on exposing the next few inches the earth swelled and a vast quantity of soil burst through the opening. This was quickly followed by a rush of water, which was so violent that it forced the man out of the frame or cell of the shield that was opposite to the opening. Mr. I. K. Brunel, who was superintending the work at the time, saw after a brief survey that it was hopeless to attempt stopping the rush of water from inside the tunnel, and ordered the men to retire. In a letter to the directors of the Company young Brunel thus describes the scene which followed

THE THAMES TUNNEL.

and led to the loss of several lives. Evidently he and the three men to whom he alludes had been the last to linger in the rear.

"At this moment the agitation of the air by the rush of the water was such as to extinguish all the lights, and the water had gained the height of the middle of our waists. I was at that moment giving directions to the three men in what manner they ought to proceed in the dark to effect their escape, when they and I were knocked down and covered by a part of the timber stage. I struggled under water for some time, and at length extricated myself from the stage ; and by swimming and being forced by the water I gained the eastern arch, where I got a better footing, and was enabled by laying hold of the railway rope to pause a little, in the hope of encouraging the men who had been knocked down at the same time with myself. This I endeavoured to do by calling to them. Before I reached the shaft the water had risen so rapidly that I was out of my depth, and therefore swam to the visitors' stairs—the stairs of the workmen being occupied by those who had so far escaped. My knee was so injured by the timber stage, that I could scarcely swim or get up the stairs, but the rush of the water carried me up the shaft. The three men who had been knocked down with me were unable to extricate themselves, and I am grieved to say they are lost; and I believe also two old men and one young man in other parts of the work."

The scene must have been very terrible. Eighteen men were at one time struggling for their lives, some of them being taken out of the water in a fainting state, and all in one of exhaustion. The roar of the flood which poured through the tunnel and up the steps was deafening, and the distress of the wives and relatives of the workmen who hastened to the spot heart-rending.

This calamity, so much more serious than the former ones, was of course disheartening to the Company who had furnished the money for the undertaking, though Brunel never lost faith in himself. The first thing to be done was to mend the rent in the bed of the river; and this was accomplished by dropping down four thousand tons of soil, chiefly clay in bags. When the water was sufficiently cleared away for the engineer to examine the Tunnel he had at least the satisfaction of seeing the work uninjured by the trial it had encountered, and in all respects as substantial as ever. Nevertheless his anguish of mind was very great, for there seemed no possibility of proceeding with his work, the darling hope of his mind.

From the first there had been a host of people who were incredulous as to the possibility of the work ever being completed; and to them every disaster had been a sort of triumph. One acquaintance of Brunel's had gone so far as to say he would " eat the shield if ever it came out on the Middlesex side of the river," and even in general society the Tunnel was a subject of conversation on which people differed, very often with all the warmth of partisans. But now it was the general opinion that the case was hopeless. The Company were in despair, and the work was perforce stopped for want of funds.

For seven weary years no stroke of work was done; but though the engineer was past the prime of life, and though his many successes might well have made him content with the fame he had won, he never faltered in his aim, or relaxed his endeavours to complete the Tunnel. His unflagging energies were rewarded. In January, 1835, the work was renewed, Government having consented to advance the necessary funds. But the progress was more slow and difficult than ever, chiefly in consequence of the saturation of the soil from the former inundations. In fact the bed of the river had constantly to be artificially made solid in advance of the shield, and then time given for it to settle. The old shield also had been injured by the water and had to be replaced by a new one—a difficult, and perilous operation, as may be understood when we consider that it alone supported above, and kept back in front the immense pressure of the river and its bed.

So difficult indeed was this undertaking considered that again Brunel had to encounter all the discouragement of friends and acquaintances, the prevailing opinion of engineers even being that the " thing was impracticable." Yet the

Tunnel could not proceed until this "impracticable" thing was accomplished. No doubt they meant well, but really people for the most part behaved as if Brunel were engaged on some wasteful work which ought to be thwarted and hindered by breaking his spirit—hurling at him

> "the bitter taunt and jest
> That Folly, in its mischievous unrest,
> Seizes with vacant laugh, and blindly flings
> At dazzling genius on her soaring wings."

But the so-called "impracticable" was accomplished : the new shield replaced its predecessor without any disturbance of the ground, or any fatal accident. Brunel's spirit was not broken, though there is too much reason to fear his bodily health suffered from the strain to which it was subjected. During the seven years from January, 1835, to the time the Tunnel was completed he never slept more than two hours at a time.

Lady Brunel herself told me of their way of life. They resided at Rotherhithe, near the shaft, and every two hours through day and night a sample of the earth excavated was submitted to

the engineer for examination, and according to
its character were the written instructions given
for the next two hours of work. At night there
were writing materials always ready in his bed-
room, and a bell was so hung as to ring near the
bed. There was also machinery arranged in the
nature of a lift by means of which the sample
of soil ascended, and by which in return the
letter of instructions was conveyed.

Think of this broken rest going on month
after month and year after year! After a time
indeed the habit of waking every two hours was
formed, and Lady Brunel assured me that for
months after the Tunnel was completed, she and
her husband found it impossible to sleep for a
greater length of time; but nevertheless it
must have been a great trial to a man in the
decline of life. For it was not merely that he
had to awake and then go to sleep again; but
he had to arise and exercise his most wide-awake
faculties, the life and death of his devoted workmen, and all the momentous issues of failure or
success depending on the sagacity of his instructions.

Although the Government had advanced money for the work of the Tunnel to proceed, the expenses were so heavy and progress was necessarily so slow, that Brunel had much anxiety about the money that would still be required being forthcoming. Indeed, the Lords of the Treasury at one time declined making further advances without the sanction of Parliament. Fortunately, however, the committee which was appointed decided that the work should not be abandoned for want of funds, and all went on satisfactorily till August, 1837, when another irruption occurred, though without such sad consequences as the last. Still the water rose to within seven feet of the crown of the arch; but there had been time to make the work secure, and the men were able to retire in an orderly manner along a platform which in view of such a possible emergency Brunel had had constructed a few weeks previously.

When the water was coming in, a boat had been used to convey materials for stopping up the frames, and after the men had retired, two or three of the assistant engineers were curious to see as closely as they could the state of the works and began using the boat for that purpose. After passing the six hundred feet mark in the tunnel the line attached to the boat ran out, and they returned to lengthen it. To this circumstance, under Divine Providence, they owed their lives, for while they were lengthening the rope the water surged, and it was calculated that not less than a million gallons of water rushed into the tunnel in a minute.

Two other irruptions occurred, one on the 2nd of November, 1837, and the other on the 6th of March, 1838; but nevertheless so much of the work was done, and so many difficulties had been overcome, that the few who had always been hopeful of success were now confident of it, and even the incredulous and desponding for the most part ceased to predict failure.

There was, however, one more disaster to be encountered. On the 4th of April, 1840, about eight o'clock in the morning a quantity of gravel and water rushed into the frame, carrying away some of the poling-boards, and knocking the men out of the shield. The first impulse of the workmen was to run away, but finding that the water did not follow them, they gained courage and returned. By great exertions the rush of earth was stopped, though not until six thousand cubic feet of ground had fallen in to encumber the tunnel. The noise this catastrophe occasioned resembled loud thunder, and the explosive force of the falling mass extinguished the lights in the tunnel. Fortunately the accident happened at low water. Had it occurred at high tide the consequences would have been far more serious.

The diary of the engineer would show two or three more disasters which, though less important than those I have recorded, were sufficiently vexatious and retarded the work when they occurred. But on the 13th of August, 1841, Brunel passed from the Middlesex side of the river through the shield into the tunnel! It must have been to him a moment of supreme delight and triumph; and the hearty cheering of the workmen as they greeted his appearance showed how warmly they felt on the occasion. They had a right to share in the glory. We may be sure they were picked men who were entrusted with duties so important that the smallest neglect of duty, or an approach to negligence in their work would have had the most terrible consequences. Being what they were they could estimate the inventive genius, the skill, the untiring energy, the patience under difficulties and the ever watchful care of themselves which had distinguished their master.

The Tunnel was now virtually completed, though much had still to be done in making the necessary approaches before it could be profitably used. The length of the Tunnel is twelve hundred feet, and its cost was somewhere about six hundred thousand pounds; a large sum no doubt, but very much less than some of our bridges have cost; and it must be remembered that the Tunnel was constructed at a point where it would have been impossible to erect a bridge without impeding navigation.

Soon after the shield had arrived at the Wapping side of the river Brunel sent a message to the acquaintance who had promised to "eat it" if ever it arrived there: "His compliments and the shield was awaiting Mr. So-and-so's digestion, whenever he liked it for dinner," or words to that effect. " Let those laugh who win " is an old proverb, and it was Brunel's turn to laugh heartily now.

In 1841 Marc Isambard Brunel received the honour of Knighthood; a distinction he valued highly, though more I think because it made his beloved wife " Lady " than on his own account. It was in the following year that I had the pleasure and privilege of knowing them and listening to their account of early trials and romantic episodes in their lives. I had written something about the Tunnel which made them know that I was interested in all they could tell me; and though Brunel was far too great a man to be vain, he had a certain simplicity in his nature which indeed is often allied to greatness, and I think he did not conceal that the Thames Tunnel was the darling creation of his mind, and a theme of which it would be hard to weary him. I was young and they were old, but I believe I was a good listener, and full of sympathy and homage. That must have been

why they told me so much of their early life—
the French prison, and the jailor's wife—and the
long years of separation.

It was pathetic to see this old couple, who
usually sat side by side, and to hear from themselves the story of their eventful lives. One bio-
grapher has said of Sir Isambard Brunel, that if
he had not been famous as an engineer he probably would have been as a philanthropist; and
I can quite understand this opinion. I have seen
the tears on his aged cheeks, when his wife was
relating something sorrowful—and when he
has been telling something in which she was
perhaps concerned I have seen him take her
withered hand and press it to his lips. "Now
Lady Brunel," I recollect his reading from his
diary with an emphasis on the title. To have
been "knighted by our fair young Queen"—and
Victoria then was young and very fair—he felt to
be a recompense for many trials. The phrase
quoted was a familiar one in their house in Great
George Street, Westminster, occurring, as it did,
in some verses a niece of Lady Brunel's had
written on the occasion.

In 1842 Brunel, now seventy-three years of age, had a stroke of paralysis, and though to a certain degree he rallied from it, he never really recovered. His writing was no longer clear and beautiful, but showed the trembling hand of infirmity and old age. Nevertheless he was able to head a simple procession which marked the formal opening of the Thames Tunnel on the 25th of March, 1843.

Medals were struck to commemorate the event, and a few friends were admitted by ticket to witness his arrival at the shaft after passing through the Tunnel. I was of the number, being one of the first half dozen who shook hands with him on his exit from the archway, when the barriers which hitherto had kept back the public were thrown down.

How well I remember the scene! An old gentleman a little under the middle height, of a figure that is called thick-set, with a fine head and ponderous brow that seemed a weight to keep down height, walking a little in advance of his companions and leaning on a stick or umbrella. There was none of the pageantry we are apt to associate with processions—only a few gentlemen in frock-coats; but to watch them advancing from the dimly lighted archway into the bright light of a spring day, kindled warm emotions in many hearts. It was a mere ceremony, but how much it meant, and how it called to mind the troubles and trials of the last twenty years! It was an hour of triumph, but the creator of the great work was now the feeble old man fatigued and overcome by that walk of twelve hundred feet. Yet was he ever most grateful that he had been permitted to embody his idea and complete his darling scheme.

Gradually his health failed more and more, but he lived till 1849. On December the 12th of that year died Sir Marc Isambard Brunel, full of honours and beloved and respected most by those who knew him best.

He was Vice-President of the Royal Society and corresponding member of the Institute of France. He left a son and two daughters. His son, Isambard Kingdom Brunel, was also a distinguished engineer, who died only a few years ago.

After all the labour bestowed and difficulties surmounted the Thames Tunnel has never been used in exactly the manner Brunel proposed. His great work was indeed completed, but the expense of making the carriage-way approaches was found to be so great, that the necessary money was never forthcoming. Perhaps the fact that the system of railway traffic was developing in an extraordinary manner, may have made people more indifferent to the uses of the Tunnel than they would otherwise have been, and for many years it was only traversed by foot passengers. At length, in July, 1866, it was transferred to a railway company, who found it worth while to construct the necessary approaches, and to lay down rails; and for many years there has been constant traffic through the Tunnel's double archway. Thus the engineer's hope of supplying a great want, and of connecting the two shores of the Thames, has been fully realized.

Many persons, no doubt, who are rapidly whirled those twelve hundred feet by the might of the snorting "iron horse," think of the river flowing above them, and of the mighty ships whose keels may be but a few yards above their heads; but perhaps only a few of them realize the skill and energy, and inventive genius which produced a work which is still the admiration of engineers, and one of the sights of London which intelligent foreigners rarely fail to visit.

THE END.